"This is not a question of whether or not I want to sleep with you again. I do."

Sienna rolled her eyes. "Please. Don't feel the need to let me down gently. I would always prefer honesty."

"As would I." He caught her chin and tilted her face up so her body jolted with the sheer pressure of awareness. "So I am being honest with you. This is complicated, not least because of our connection through Luca and Olivia."

"What difference does that make?"

He stared down at her, his eyes probing hers, reading her, his lips parted, his body tense, and she moaned softly, because this was impossible.

"Look, Alejandro, just forget I cam̲ ̲ ̲ ̲ ̲ ̲ ̲ You're right. There are other guys ̲ ̲ ̲ ̲ ̲ ̲ ̲, other men who'll—"

It was like s̲ ̲ ̲ ̲ ̲ ̲ ̲ ̲ ̲ ̲ ̲ ̲ ̲ ̲ ̲ ̲ ̲ ̲is nostrils flare̲ ̲ ̲ ̲ ̲ ̲ ̲ ̲ ̲ ̲ ̲ ̲ ̲ ̲as right in front ̲ ̲ ̲ ̲ ̲ ̲ ̲ ̲ ̲ ̲ ̲e come in here and talk̲ ̲ ̲ ̲ ̲ ̲ ̲ ̲ ̲en—"

"You're the one ̲ ̲ ̲ ̲ ̲aid there'd be someone more suitable—"

"I was wrong." And then he was kissing her, but not like she'd ever been kissed before.

The Cinderella Sisters

From billion-dollar matches to unexpected awakenings!

Thornton-Rose sisters Olivia and Sienna look like they have everything—from the outside. But when their calculating father leaves a will demanding that in order to gain their inheritance, one of them must marry before they're twenty-five, everything seems to fall apart. Olivia steps in to take the trip down her convenient aisle. But saying "I do" may just secure both these innocents' fates...and could open them to a whole new world of passion, thanks to the gorgeous playboy bachelors they encounter!

Read Olivia and Luca's story in
Vows on the Virgin's Terms

And read Sienna and Alejandro's story in
Forbidden Nights in Barcelona

Both available now!

Clare Connelly

FORBIDDEN NIGHTS IN BARCELONA

HARLEQUIN® PRESENTS®

ISBN-13: 978-1-335-56838-0

Forbidden Nights in Barcelona

Copyright © 2022 by Clare Connelly

This edition published by arrangement with Harlequin Books S.A.

For questions and comments about the quality of this book,
please contact us at CustomerService@Harlequin.com.

Harlequin Enterprises ULC
22 Adelaide St. West, 41st Floor
Toronto, Ontario M5H 4E3, Canada
www.Harlequin.com

Printed in U.S.A.

Clare Connelly was raised in small-town Australia among a family of avid readers. She spent much of her childhood up a tree, Harlequin book in hand. Clare is married to her own real-life hero, and they live in a bungalow near the sea with their two children. She is frequently found staring into space—a surefire sign she is in the world of her characters. She has a penchant for French food and ice-cold champagne, and Harlequin novels continue to be her favorite-ever books. Writing for Harlequin Presents is a long-held dream. Clare can be contacted via clareconnelly.com or on her Facebook page.

Books by Clare Connelly

Harlequin Presents

Their Impossible Desert Match
My Forbidden Royal Fling
Crowned for His Desert Twins

A Billion-Dollar Singapore Christmas

An Heir Claimed by Christmas
No Strings Christmas
(Available from Harlequin DARE)

Signed, Sealed...Seduced

Cinderella's Night in Venice

The Cinderella Sisters

Vows on the Virgin's Terms

Visit the Author Profile page
at Harlequin.com for more titles.

PROLOGUE

Luca and Olivia's wedding celebration

'ALEJANDRO, I NEED your help.'

Luca beamed like a newly married man despite the fact his actual wedding had taken place months earlier, and this was a 'do over', to celebrate his matrimonial happiness with everyone he'd ever met—by the looks of the humming crowd, at least. And in the midst of all the exquisitely dressed wedding guests, Alejandro stood out like a sore thumb.

Not because he was dressed any differently—like most of the male guests, he wore a tuxedo. No, Alejandro stood out because of who he was, his bearing a testament to the man who'd dragged himself out of extreme poverty by his wits alone, a man who was the definition of having come from the wrong side of the tracks—and wasn't ashamed of that. Rather than hiding his heritage, he wore it like a badge of honour, a flicker of derision shaping his lips when confronted with Europe's elite—old money, who wouldn't have any idea how cruel life could be. They were his antithesis, and he relished that fact, their wealth and privilege something he despised—all the more so for knowing it was a part of *his* heritage too—a heritage—parentage—that had never wanted him, never acknowledged him.

'It's Olivia's sister, Sienna.'

Alejandro narrowed his arctic-blue eyes, following his friend's gaze until it landed on a woman in the distance, standing off to the side, alone, separate from the party swirling around them. She was as different from Olivia as was possible. Where Luca's bride was willow thin with pale blonde hair, Sienna was short, curvaceous, with pale skin and titian-red hair. Alejandro's gaze travelled the length of her body before he realised what he was doing.

'Stop that,' Luca growled. 'Before I change my mind.'

Alejandro shifted his attention back to his friend with surprising reluctance. 'What is it you want from me?'

'Olivia adores Sienna. She's very protective of her.'

Alejandro lifted a brow. 'She seems like a big girl, capable of handling herself.'

'Perhaps.'

'You don't sound convinced.'

'What I'm convinced about is wanting my bride to enjoy her second wedding more than her first. She can't do that when she's worried about Sienna.'

Once again, Alejandro regarded the red-haired woman, something like curiosity sparking inside his chest. He hadn't looked properly before. He'd simply run his eyes over her. But now, he studied her, an alabaster face with eyes that were so green they were like polished emeralds. She smiled, but Luca was right—

there was something discordant behind her eyes, sadness and hurt. Alejandro had known enough of both emotions to recognise them instantly.

Alejandro's lips formed a grim line. 'What can I do about it?'

'I'm glad you asked. I want you to entertain Sienna.'

Alejandro turned back to his friend. 'Do you mean...?'

'Absolutely not.' Fierce rejection tightened Luca's eyes. 'What do you take me for? A pimp?' He lifted a hand, palm towards Alejandro. 'In fact, I'm forbidding you from so much as touching her. She's not suitable to be one of your one-night stands, so don't go getting any ideas. She's not your type.'

Alejandro stroked his jaw. 'You're *forbidding* me?' he murmured aloud, fighting an urge to point out that forbidden fruit always tasted so much sweeter.

'Yes. All I'm asking is that you rescue Sienna from their godawful mother.'

Alejandro's smile was cynical. 'And what is so awful about her?' His eyes landed on the woman across the party, stunningly beautiful, far younger in appearance than her age, and utterly aware of that fact.

'That would take far longer than we have.'

'And you're anxious to get back to your bride.'

'My wife,' Luca confirmed with a beaming grin. 'Yes.' He considered his best friend, as though weighing something up delicately, then leaned a little closer, lowering his tone despite the fact they were quite separate from the other guests. 'Angelica, their mother, has spent the day berating Sienna. Olivia has held her tongue, but just barely, and I am truly concerned that if there is one more incident, my lovely, kind wife will turn into a dragon and breathe fire over everyone.'

'Would that be a bad thing?'

'Actually, it would probably be a very good thing: Angelica could do with being put in her place, if you ask me.' He sighed. 'But Olivia is too sweet, and she would hate herself almost immediately. Which is why I need you to stay between Sienna and Angelica so Olivia doesn't have to lose her cool.'

There was no one on earth who meant more to Alejandro than Luca. No one he could rely on, no one he trusted. Those feelings were mutual. Luca was the only person who understood what Alejandro's life had been like *before*. He knew about Alejandro's mother, he knew about her profession, her life, her death, and he knew what home life had been like—why Alejandro was an expert at street fighting, because he'd had to become one, in order to survive. There was no one else on earth Alejandro had allowed to see and understand those parts of him, and Luca had shared the same depth of himself with Alejandro. Theirs was a friendship Alejandro would never jeopardise.

'Fine,' Alejandro agreed, though not without misgivings. He wasn't a babysitter.

'Thank you.' Luca flicked a relieved smile at his friend. 'I think I can remember how to play that part.' After all, it was just one night, just one woman. What could go wrong?

CHAPTER ONE

'YOU LOOK AS though you'd rather be anywhere but here.'

Sienna grimaced even before she turned to address the voice that had spoken, wishing she had been more successful at hiding her feelings and thoughts, wishing she had done a better job of looking as everyone wanted her to.

Naturally, she intended to deny the claim until she was blue in the face, but any idea of speaking flew from her mind the minute her eyes landed on the man who possessed the voice. It wasn't as if he was the first handsome man she'd seen in her life, but, then again, handsome was a manifestly insufficient word to describe him.

Handsome was a word that was safe and ordinary, mild and run-of-the-mill, and none of those adjectives could be safely applied to the man who stood beside her, quirked lips that were moulded with obvious cynicism, eyes the exact colour of the sky at midday, deep blue, flecked with silver and black, so she stared into them and felt as though she were falling through space. His face was perfectly symmetrical, his jaw squared, as though shaped from stone, his brows thick and a dark brown, to match his slightly waved hair. He wore a tuxedo but he didn't really—at least, not in the ordinary sense. The tuxedo was simply a prop, a costume, something donned for the wedding—it couldn't hide his raw strength, his masculine virility, and the way it pulsed from him with an almost magnetic strength.

'Weddings aren't my scene either,' he commented with a twist of his mouth, so her eyes dropped lower without her consent, tracing the outline of his lips until her tummy flipped and flopped and she had to wrench her eyes away or she was honestly terrified she might do something completely crazy and *kiss* him.

Her breath felt hot, trapped in her lungs, and her eyes seemed to dance with stars. She sought refuge in the crowd, scanning the room looking for something, anything, to anchor her to reality, only to clash with her mother's gaze, and the disapproval on her beautiful face as she scrutinised Sienna's appearance for the hundredth time that hour.

Out of the frying pan, into the fire...

'Do you speak English?' He attempted once more, and now, despite the coil that was tightening in the pit of her stomach, she found a small smile, flashing it at him with no idea of how it transformed her face, making her eyes sparkle and pressing a deep dimple into either cheek. Despite many attempts over the years, Sienna had never learned to hide her cheeky, impish nature from her features, and it beamed out of her now.

'I do.' She didn't add that she also spoke several other languages—just managing two words had been an impressive feat.

'Then you're being diplomatic regarding the wedding?'

'Perhaps generally, but not on this occasion. My sister's the bride.' She gestured towards Olivia, who was being held by her husband, dancing softly, slowly, in the middle of the room. 'I'm very happy for her.'

'I can tell.'

Sienna's eyes widened in surprise and then she laughed, a soft, musical sound that had Alejandro standing imperceptibly taller, his eyes narrowing as they raked her face, then briefly dipped to the hint of cleavage exposed by the maid of honour dress.

His inspection was fleeting, but impossible to miss, and heat, a heat she'd never before known, flooded Sienna's body so she had to swallow in an attempt to douse it. But it felt so good! Even as she wrestled for control, she wanted to relish this sensation, to glory in the way her body was stirring in response to his—a total stranger. It felt naughty and nice, all at once.

'Are you always so honest?'

'Yes.'

Her mother would say it wasn't polite to pry, but Sienna was famously bad at following her mother's advice, and found herself asking, 'Why?'

'What is the alternative? To lie?'

'No. To be socially appropriate?'

'Appropriateness is overrated,' he said with a lift of his broad shoulders, so she was torn between a bubble of laughter and a moan of attraction. Thank God, her body settled on the former.

'How do you know the happy couple?' she asked, a

hint of worry briefly creasing her eyes as she looked at Olivia and Luca once more.

'Luca is my oldest friend.'

'How come you weren't his best man, then?'

'Now who's being direct?'

'Is it a secret?'

'Not at all.'

'So?'

'Weddings aren't my thing either. It would have been hypocritical for me to stand up there beside him today.'

'Even for thirty minutes?'

'I don't believe in marriage. I don't respect the institution. I don't accept the necessity. Frankly, there couldn't be a worse choice for best man than me. And so I politely declined.'

'But he did ask you?'

The man's dark head dipped forward. 'And with no real expectation of success. Luca knows how I feel about things.'

Heat was a torrent in her veins. 'What did you say your name was?'

'I didn't.'

She poked out her tongue. 'You're very literal as well.'

His grin was slow to spread and delightful to behold. Sparks ignited in her bloodstream. Uh oh. That was probably not a good thing.

'Are you asking my name, *bonita*?'

'I suppose I was,' she responded archly.

'Alejandro.'

The way he pronounced it sent a shiver down her spine, like stepping from the shadows and into sunshine on a cool autumnal afternoon. She stayed right where she was, letting the effect of the word wash over her, the guttural way he'd spoken the middle syllable an aphrodisiac she couldn't ignore.

Aphrodisiac?

Since when?

Aphrodisiacs weren't exactly arrows in Sienna's quiver. It wasn't as if she went around talking to handsome men every night of the week, nor was she remotely familiar with the experiences of what one man's full attention could do to her body. It was as if she were being gradually set alight, blood cell by blood cell, until she could hardly think straight.

'And you are?'

She blinked, blankly. 'I'm…what do you mean?'

Now it was his turn to laugh, a short, hoarse sound that spelled disaster for her already weakened grip on control—and, she feared, reality. Because why in the world would a man like this be talking to her? And even though he was talking, there was no way he was feeling the deluge of fascination and desire that was running rampant through her.

'Your name,' he prompted silkily, holding out his hand to shake. 'What is it?'

'Oh. I'm Sienna,' she mumbled, colour rising in her cheeks. How she hated that! When Olivia blushed, she looked beautiful and coquettish, like some kind of ethereal fairy creature in need of protection. Whereas, when Sienna blushed, with her red hair and freckles, she was more like an homage to a Titian palette after a particularly fruitful afternoon, all blotchy and messed.

'Sienna.' He repeated her name, slowly and tinged

with his accent—Spanish?—so a thousand fireworks burst in her belly. His hand moved closer and, of its own volition, hers extended slowly, curiously, as though the simple act of touching hand to hand heralded some kind of unavoidable disaster.

Little could she know.

'Would you like to dance?'

'Dance?' she repeated, staring at the makeshift dance floor—a terrace in Rome strung with fairy lights and surrounded by potted plants filled with night-flowering jasmine that created a heavenly fragrance. A sinking feeling dropped through her stomach. 'Dancing' implied grace and coordination, two things Sienna generally felt she lacked. And yet, it also meant closeness. Touching. A reason to run her hands over this man's muscular torso, to feel—

Oh, for heaven's sake. He's not asking you to take him to bed.

And what would she say if he did? Disastrously, more heat bloomed in her cheeks, so she squeezed her eyes shut, hoping to blot him and the whole world out.

'It is not rocket science,' he said, close enough for the words to brush her ear. 'I can show you.'

He knew. He knew she had no experience. He knew she was nervous. Yeah, well, of course he did! It wasn't as if she could be mistaken for a suave, sophisticated socialite, the kind of woman for whom events like this were run of the mill.

Just be yourself.

Olivia's earlier advice ran through her, but instead of giving her comfort, it brought a smile to Sienna's face. Being herself would have meant wearing jeans and an oversized sweater, and her mutt, Starbuck, firmly planted by her side. She turned to face him, then wished she hadn't when she was assaulted anew by his devastating good looks.

'I don't really dance,' she explained, but despite the demurral her eyes ravaged his face then dropped lower, to the chest she was aching to feel, to understand if it was quite so firm as she imagined.

'You don't like to dance?'

How could she know? Apart from a few school parties, which she'd spent glued to the wall like some kind of Grecian statue, or ferrying drinks for people in the hope no one would notice how awkward and out of place she felt, Sienna couldn't have said.

'I should—' She cast about for an excuse, a reason to leave him, even though her feet wanted to stay firmly planted right where they were. She waved a hand vaguely in the direction of her bestie, Gertie, across the space. Her eyes followed the direction in which her hand pointed, and so the last thing she expected was for him to touch her.

Not just to touch her, but to lace his fingers through hers in an act that was, for Sienna, so intimate her breath hitched in her throat beneath the stars of this ancient city. Everything inside her seemed to shift. She whirled around to face him, lips parted, eyes wide, and a bold sense of daring gripped her, a rush of fearlessness that made her want to tip headlong into whatever madness was whispering on the sultry summer evening's air.

He was watching her through veiled eyes, impossible to see. Unlike Sienna, he was a master at concealing what he was thinking and feeling.

Stop overreacting.

'Come and dance with me, *bonita*. One song.'

His fingers were warm and strong, his hand much larger than hers. She stared down at the contact, her pulse heavy in her throat, so she was conscious of every quiver and rushed beat.

'Okay,' she said after a beat. *Be yourself.* 'But don't blame me when your feet need to be amputated because I've trodden on them so many times.'

His smile set her soul on fire. 'Deal.' And then, because he clearly specialised in Moves That Could Shock Her, Alejandro lifted her hand to his lips and brushed a kiss across it, searing every single cell in her body. How could she feel aflame at the same time a tingly shivery feeling ran along her back? Contradictions flooded her—she was reluctant to dance with him even when it felt like the most important thing to her as well.

She hadn't been exaggerating. Sienna Thornton-Rose was not a natural dancer, and, for some reason he couldn't put his finger on, he found that…intriguing. He found *her* intriguing, in ways he'd probably be better able to analyse if her body weren't so close to his, every little jerk of her legs bringing her voluptuous curves nearer, breasts that were so rounded he found his palms aching to lift up and feel them, to appraise their weight and fullness for himself, to admire them naked, to take one of her nipples in his mouth, to—

She's not suitable to be one of your one-night stands.

Alejandro ground his teeth together, forcing himself to look across the dance floor to where Olivia and

Luca were dancing. Luca was completely wrapped up in his bride; he wasn't looking at Alejandro and Sienna.

Because he trusts you.

So? He wasn't planning to do anything to betray that trust. But Luca had asked Alejandro to distract Sienna, to show her a good time, and it was quite clear that she was *not* having a good time. Yet.

Something like adrenaline rushed his body as he put his hands on her hips, those huge green eyes of hers widening like saucers as she stared up at him, her long lashes, painted a dark black, blinking as a frown tilted her full lower lip downwards. She was nothing like the kind of woman he usually dated, but there was something about her that was making Alejandro's breath heavy in his lungs. He was conscious of all of himself and all of her. Did the freckles that leaped opportunistically across the bridge of her nose appear anywhere else on her body? Were her lashes naturally the same colour as her hair, a deep, rich, rusty red? And the hair on her sex?

Hell. Having been told she was off limits was driving him crazy. All Alejandro could think about was a rising tide of desire rampaging his system. But his life was about control and he refused to succumb to the weakness of temptation—not when Luca had been so explicit.

'You have to relax,' he encouraged, even when pressure was building inside him like a coil. 'Feel the rhythm of the music. Let it touch something in your soul.'

'I'd relax a little more if you were a little less like a Spanish-deity-cum-Hollywood-star brought to life,' she snapped, and then flushed, as though she were embarrassed, but her eyes stayed locked to his, something unapologetic and addictive in their depths.

Why did he find her admission so pleasing? After all, Alejandro was well aware of his impact on women. He was a renowned bachelor for a reason, able to take his pick of most women at most events. And yet, her unsophisticated compliment, her irritation at finding him attractive, made him want to tease her.

To tempt her.

Oh, *mierda*. He really needed to think of Luca, but the truth was his best friend was the last thing he wanted in his mind in that moment.

'Is dancing with a deity not on your bucket list?' he prompted, bringing his body closer, even as his brain berated him for such weakness.

He felt the air whoosh out of her lungs, felt it brush his cheek, and immediately he wondered about how she'd sound when she was coming, how her breath would rush over him as she cried his name at the top of her lungs... He held back a curse as he began to stiffen in his pants, the fabric at his crotch a welcome constraint given that he was dancing with his best friend's newly minted sister-in-law.

'Surprisingly not,' she said, stiffly.

'Relax,' he reminded her, and when she didn't, he lifted one hand to her chin, tilting her face to his, holding it there so he could look into her eyes. 'Don't look away,' he commanded, so used to being obeyed in every aspect of his life that it didn't occur to him for one moment she would be any different. He slowly lowered his hand, watching her the whole time, bringing his hand back to her hip, and then moving her in time with the music. Only it wasn't really the music he was synchronising her with, so much as the rhythmic rushing of his blood, the building of awareness deep within him, an ache he would normally know he was within hours of satisfying.

Not tonight, he reminded himself forcibly. *Not with her.*

The maid of honour dress was exceptionally beautiful. He'd noticed that when she'd walked into the church. Unlike other weddings he'd attended, where the bride had sought to outshine all in attendance, Olivia had clearly chosen a dress designed to flatter her sister with every detail. From the deep emerald green that emphasised the mystery of Sienna's eyes, to the floaty material that clung to her full breasts like a second skin then fell loose and flowing to her knees, so Alejandro wanted to bunch the chiffon fabric in his fists and lift it, to slip his hand beneath the hem and feel the curve of her bottom, to—

Cristo. He was losing the plot. Luca would kill him if he continued down this path. Hell, he'd kill himself for betraying his friend.

'You're very good at this.' Her words pulled him back to the present.

'Dancing?'

'Casting women under a spell.'

Her honesty tugged at him. Amused him. But also stirred something he hadn't felt in a long time, a protective instinct that reminded him forcibly of nights worrying for his mother, wishing there were something he could do—

'Is that what I'm doing?'

'Oh, don't ask that. It's even more embarrassing if you're not trying.'

He laughed, aware of the effect the sound had on her, of the way she stopped dancing and simply stared at him. Temptation had never been such a force to be grappled with as it was then. Her lips were so full and sweetly pink, they demanded to be kissed. Not just kissed, but ravished beneath the demands of his own mouth, to be drawn between his teeth, to be dominated completely.

'I'm simply dancing with a beautiful young woman,' he said with a shrug of his shoulders.

It was as if she'd been slapped. Sienna's hands dropped to her sides and she took a step back from him, her face paling so the cheeky little freckles stood out much more.

'I should go and check on my aunts, make sure they have drinks.' Her smile was tight, lacking any of the spontaneity and mirth he'd seen earlier, and it felt as though he'd been cast to the dark side of the moon. He told himself he should be relieved—he needed space to get a grip on the attraction that was humming between them—but he wasn't. 'Excuse me.'

Before he could shake himself back to the here and now and reach out and catch her hand once more, she was gone, slipping through the crowd, spine ramrod-straight, as though she had something to prove—to him and the world. He watched her walk away, a frown on his face and an ache forming, deep, low in his gut.

CHAPTER TWO

BEAUTIFUL? SHE FUMED as she slipped away from the party altogether, towards the edge of the Tiber river, dancing slowly beneath the full moon. Right up until that moment, he'd almost had her. She'd believed his practised seduction. She'd believed that he wanted to dance with her. That he saw her as she was.

Which was *not* beautiful.

She wasn't being down on herself, she was simply being honest. Objectively speaking, it was easy to face that reality when your mother was Angelica Thornton-Rose and your sister was Olivia. It was impossible to have any false hope about your own beauty. She was the thorn amongst two roses, or the fluffy little rust-coloured duck between two elegant, gracious swans, and she'd long ago given up hope of some kind of magical transformation turning her into one of them. She never would be, and she didn't need to be lied to and flattered by some guest at the party. Even one who made her feel as though she wanted to—well, suffice it to say, Sienna was fighting impulses she'd never known before.

She stared out at the river and with each fast, knotty turn of the water she quelled her own blood's rushing, drawing herself back to reality even when the fantasy of what she'd just experienced was so very, very tempting.

'Have you seen Sisi?' Olivia's beautiful face was placid, but her eyes showed worry.

Alejandro looked at the bride, trying to spot any similarities between the two, and failing. Olivia's face was heart-shaped and symmetrical, her eyes wide-spaced and a deep blue, her hair naturally so fair it was almost white. There were no fascinating freckles on her nose, no flashes of the ocean in her eyes, and her lips were dull and flat when compared to the full, tempting pout of Sienna's.

'My sister,' Olivia clarified, mistaking his lack of response for non-comprehension.

'We thought you were dancing with her.' Luca's voice held a warning, and also a plea.

'Don't worry about it,' Olivia murmured, craning her slender neck as her eyes ran over the guests of the party. 'I'm sure she's here somewhere.'

Alejandro didn't need Luca's pointed stare to offer to go and look for her. Even as he said the words, excitement bubbled up inside his chest. 'I'll find her, if you'd like.'

'No, it's fine. I should go and check on her, make sure she's—'

'Let him do it,' Luca urged. 'You know Sienna hates it when you worry.'

Alejandro suspected, in fact, that Olivia didn't need to worry. Not as much as she did. For all that he'd only known Sienna a matter of minutes—ten at most—he was good at judging people, and he could feel her strength from a mile away. He didn't think Sienna needed to be found to be sure she was all right, but that didn't stop him from wanting to find her. Only his motivations were far from altruistic.

'It is your wedding. It's the least I can do, given I shirked best man duties,' he said with a grim smile, feeling like a wolf in sheep's clothing. Luca's grateful expression made it even worse. What would his friend say if he knew that Alejandro wanted to seek Sienna out for the pleasure of her proximity alone? That his offer had very little to do with Luca's concerns?

'Ah. So you are still here.'

Just when Sienna was getting herself back into a normal sinus rhythm, Alejandro—or the voice of him— swirled through the balmy Roman air towards her, wrapping around her belly first then spreading and popping through her entire body. She turned slowly, because she needed time to steel herself for this—as hard as it had been to grapple with his ridiculous charisma in the middle of the wedding party, doing so here, alone, in a quiet space away from the restaurant, with only the river and the moon and the ancient ghosts of this spectacular city for company, she feared his god-like abilities would overwhelm her.

Well, duh.

He held a flute of champagne towards her and she reached out, curving her fingers around it instinctively—after all, that was what one did with proffered drinks—only he didn't immediately retract his hand, so their fingers brushed and held and it was as though every star in the heavens had poured its energy into her fingertips. She buzzed all over.

'Thank you.' She jerked the glass back towards herself, lifting it to her lips and drinking, quickly, in a need to extinguish the fires that were ravaging her central nervous system.

He shrugged with indolent relaxation, moving closer, until he was right beside her, just ever so slightly too close, so she was wrapped up in him—his exotic, masculine fragrance, the heat of his body and the sheer magnetic aura of the man, so that she had to fight to stop from sinking into him.

She held the glass with two hands and turned back to the river, no longer able to pretend her heat rate was anything like calm.

'You ran away from me.'

There was no point in denying it. 'I needed some space.'

'You're not enjoying yourself.'

The problem was, she *had* been enjoying herself, a little too much. 'It's been a long day.' Starting with the horrors of getting ready for the wedding with their mother, hearing her wax lyrical about Olivia's beauty and Sienna's failings—as though Sienna hadn't made her peace with the genetic lottery years earlier!

'Couldn't you have chosen a dress for Sienna that didn't make her look like a chubby leprechaun?'

She was used to her mother's taunts, but she'd been feeling so good about herself in the floaty princess gown, and so the sting had been acute.

'Where are you from?'

She told herself she asked the question to be polite, but the truth was she didn't want him to leave again.

'Barcelona.'

'You speak English very well.'

'I went to school there.'

'Ah. Where exactly?'

He named one of the most prestigious schools in the country, on the outskirts of London. She tilted her head, studying him thoughtfully.

'Yes?' he prompted, his blue eyes stirring plumes of desire—for the feeling was now unmistakable, despite her lack of personal experience.

There was no sense lying to him. She sipped her champagne, needing the rush of flavour, the calming effect of the bubbles. 'You don't seem like a public school snob,' she said and then offered a little grimace of apology.

'Don't I?'

She shook her head, and at the same time a gentle breeze carried off the Tiber, so her hair brushed her cheek. His hand lifted, catching it and tucking it slowly behind her ear. But even once the hair was restrained, he didn't drop his hand, and she stood perfectly, completely still, not wanting to breathe lest she dislodge the contact.

'Why not?' Had he moved closer? She was sure he had. Or had that been her after all? Their legs were brushing, and if she breathed in or out too quickly the force would jut her breasts forward, to touch his chest. The very idea made her nipples tingle against the soft fabric of her bra and a swirl of temptation moved through her.

'Sienna?' He was asking her to elaborate, and yet it felt as though the question meant something else. As though he were asking—to kiss her?

Breath rushed from between her teeth at the very idea. Her lips parted and she stared up into his eyes, the moonlight hitting them at the perfect angle to cast them not as blue but as silver, and so mysterious she was sure that every fairy tale ever written had somehow had its genesis in their depths. Of its own volition, one of her hands rose and pressed to his chest, so tentative, so uncertain, but the moment her fingers connected with the fabric of his shirt she felt a rush of rightness, that this was just exactly what she'd been wanting to do since he'd first approached her. His body was warm, and his chest, beneath her gently exploring hand, was as hard as a rock, just as she'd speculated it would be. Her touch was light, but its effect was not. His cheeks darkened with a slash of colour and something fired in his expression—hesitation. Doubt. But also, she was sure of it, desire.

And yet his hesitation was obvious and, for Sienna, it was easy to believe that it had been born out of disgust for her. Pity even. How could anyone desire her when there were the Olivias of the world?

'Thank you for the drink,' she mumbled, taking a step backwards, wondering at the madness that had overtaken her in daring to hope he might be as attracted to her as she was to him. *Fool.* It was the romance of the wedding ceremony. Nothing more.

His brows drew closer together and she held her breath, wondering if she'd got it wrong. Maybe he'd close the gap, lift her hand back to his chest. And maybe merry little pigs would fly right by the nearby Castel Sant'Angelo.

'Luca is one of my oldest friends,' he said quietly, the words flattened of emotion, and in his eyes there was a faraway look, as though he wasn't really talking to her so much as to himself.

'You mentioned that already.' She swallowed past a throat that was suddenly thick.

His eyes pinned hers and then seemed to lance right through her. He didn't speak, nor did she. Not at first. She wasn't capable of it. Her body was vibrating and the longer he stared at her, the more she began to tremble, to feel as though she were both floating and sinking.

'Did you meet him at school?' It was a valiant attempt to grab hold of something normal, to tether herself to a form of reality and normality. 'I know he went to a school in the UK, for a time. Was that where—' She was babbling, and cut herself off short with a slight grimace.

He was staring at her as though he'd never seen a woman before, and maybe he hadn't. Not one like her— wild, untamed, folksy rather than elegant, more at home by the fire with a good book or riding a horse across the countryside than somewhere like this. She lifted her champagne to her lips, took a sip, then clutched the glass in front of her, searching for something to say that would keep him here while simultaneously resigning herself to the likelihood that he would leave again.

'Yes.' A simple statement that confused her completely.

'Yes, what?'

He took a step, closing the distance between them,

and Sienna expelled a breath she hadn't realised she'd been holding.

'Yes.' His hands curled around the champagne flute, removing it from her grip. She dropped her gaze, wondering if he was going to put it down. 'That is where I met Luca.' There was only the glow of moonlight, casting his face into angles and planes, but his eyes shone. With determination? He took a sip of her champagne, and the simple act of his having shared her glass was so intimate, she trembled inside.

But it was nothing compared to what came next. A moment after filling his mouth with champagne, he dropped his lips to hers, spilling the liquid into her mouth in an act that was so erotic she moaned, and her knees turned to liquid, so her only options were to melt to the ground or cling on to him for dear life. She chose the latter, wrapping her arms around his neck as she swallowed the champagne and his tongue took its place, plundering her mouth, dancing with her tongue, kissing her in a way she'd never been kissed before. This couldn't possibly compare to the inexperienced fumbles of the various boyfriends she'd had over the years—and they had been boys, not men, not lovers, nothing like this.

Heat stole into her cheeks as the effect of his touch, the dominance of his kiss, the way his huge body made her feel delicate and fragile, made her feel feminine as she'd never felt before, as his kiss changed something essential inside her. She could hardly breathe and she didn't care—other things sustained her now, like the pressing need for *more*, for all of him. She yearned to be closer, to have—to feel—she didn't know what, only his kiss wasn't enough, no matter how sensational it was. Fireworks were dancing all around her, a localised effect, just between him and her, and their private little piece of the banks of the Tiber. His hand caught the back of her head, weaving through her thick hair, holding her head still, deepening the kiss as his body pushed forward, so she moved with him, stepping backwards and backwards again until her back connected with the stone balustrade that guarded the river.

And now she understood the origins of the expression to be caught between a rock and a hard place because she was, quite literally, and it was the most sublime form of pleasure she'd ever known. His hardness pressed to her sex, unmistakable, and she moaned softly beneath him, as his hand reached down, brushing her thigh, lifting her skirt, coming around to cup her bottom and push her forward all at once, holding her tight against him as he kissed her until she saw stars and oblivion.

It wasn't enough to be kissed by him though, it wasn't enough to be touched like this. She needed to touch and feel too. She pushed up, scrambling to sit on the edge of the balustrade, so he could stand between her legs, legs that she wrapped around his waist and hooked at the ankles, and now it was Alejandro that moaned, the sound trapped low in his throat, followed by a coarse Spanish curse, and then he dragged his kiss lower, to her decolletage, working his mouth along her collarbone before flicking the indent at the centre, then roaming lower, to the gentle valley of cleavage hinted at by the beautiful dress Olivia had chosen.

She tilted her head back, staring at the sky, wondering if this was a dream, or a wish come true. Wondering how she, Sienna, had suddenly become the kind of girl that this sort of thing could happen to. Wondering… and enjoying…the perfection of his mouth as he drew it back to hers, kissing her again, pulling her close to him, his hips moving to simulate—she could only guess, but she suspected—sex, and, oh, how she wanted this man to take her here, now, with the river their only witness. The party might as well have been a thousand miles away. It would be her first time, but would that matter? Not to Sienna. She wasn't saving her virginity for anyone. It was an inconvenience, a by-product of her upbringing, little more.

The idea took hold of her, digging into her mind, so her fingers reached for his belt, unfastening it, and she was so sure of what she wanted that her hands didn't even tremble. She had never been surer of anything in her life. Pleasure was the wind at her back, propelling her actions, guiding her, driving any doubt from her mind. How could she doubt when she could feel? His desire, his want, his obvious need? It was a strength and fire she hadn't known was missing until now, but as her hands reached inside his pants and curved around his arousal she felt a burst of triumph, of womanly knowledge, an ancient, feminine understanding of her power, and she smiled like the cat who'd got the cream, pulling away from him, her breath ragged, her eyes holding a challenge and an invitation.

Holy hell.

He stared down at her as though awakening from a dream—the best dream he'd ever had, a dream that had crept up on him out of nowhere, that had dragged him into its centre before he realised what was happening. Or was it a nightmare? A nightmare because this was *exactly* what Luca had told him not to do, exactly what he'd sworn to himself he could control? His best friend deserved more from him, damn it, and Alejandro wasn't the kind of man to ignore his sense of loyalty—no matter the temptation.

'Now who is casting a spell over whom?' he muttered, reaching down and dislodging her grip from his throbbing, painfully tightened cock, staring at her with a sinking feeling that he was putting an end to something that was overwhelming him with the power of his need. But need be damned. He wasn't going to be this man. For Luca to have been so strenuous in warning Alejandro away from Sienna, there must have been good reason. And he could see that clearly for himself: she was *nice*. Too nice for him. Gentle and sweet and kind, exactly the kind of woman he avoided like the plague, because nice women were ripe to being hurt by men like him, and he refused to be an instrument of pain. Luca knew that, and so he'd warned Alejandro. None of which was Sienna's fault.

'I—' Disappointment and surprise crossed her features and then, unmistakably, hurt, so he wanted to undo the last thirty seconds, replace her hand on his arousal, and kiss her again until she was moaning beneath him, those sweet, soft little noises just exactly what he wanted to hear right now.

'I got carried away,' he said, quietly, the understatement shaming him.

'We both did.' She stepped down from the balustrade, ignoring the hand he held out in a gesture of help, fixing him with a cool stare that was only slightly undermined by the shaking of her lower lip.

He watched as she straightened her dress—it didn't even occur to him to turn away until much later—and the way her hands ran over her body, making sure everything was in place, was its own special torment, because while she touched her body all he could think about was his own hands following that exact course. He balled fists at his sides then thrust them into his pockets.

'Listen, Sienna—' But what could he say? How could he explain that he'd made a promise to his friend not to touch her? How could he say that without making her feel like a piece of meat two men had negotiated over? Anger flared in his belly—Luca had asked him for a favour and it hadn't occurred to Alejandro to mind, until he'd met Sienna. Now, the idea of being prohibited from being with her was burning through him like acid.

'Excuse me.' Her tone was like ice, her imminent departure making the decision for him. 'I think I hear my mother calling for me.'

She'd made up the excuse to get away, before she evaporated into a cloud of embarrassment or, worse, begged him to kiss her again, because she liked it so bloody much, but the moment she rejoined the wedding party Angelica wrapped her hand around Sienna's wrist, halting her in her tracks.

'There you are,' Angelica hissed. 'What in the world have you been doing? You look like you've been dragged through the bush backwards.' Disapproval lined Angelica's beautiful, slightly lined face as she reached up and began to neaten Sienna's unruly hair. 'Honestly, the best stylist in Europe worked on you all afternoon and this is what you end up with?'

Sienna felt as though she'd just had a head-on collision with a runaway freight train.

'Leave it, Mother. It's fine.'

'It is *not* fine,' Angelica responded curtly. 'This is your sister's wedding and for whatever reason—charity, I suppose—she's chosen *you* to be her maid of honour. You can't possibly be photographed with her looking like this.'

Sienna ground her teeth together, so used to her mother's harsh put-downs that she barely flinched now. 'I was beyond the terrace. It was breezy.'

'This is useless. We'll have to go and fix it in the ladies' room.'

'Mother?' Sienna reached up and grabbed her mother's wrist, pulling it away from her hair. 'I can do it. This is Olivia's wedding. You shouldn't disappear. Stay with the guests. Mingle.'

It was exactly the right thing to suggest—and not by accident. Sienna knew enough of her mother's vanity and preening instincts to know that what she wanted, most of all, was to be the centre of attention herself— and if she couldn't manage that, to get as close as possible to it. Olivia was where the spotlight shone brightest, not Sienna.

'Fix yourself up,' Angelica insisted, as a parting shot. 'This is not the time to show the world the real you.'

Sienna sighed, so her hair lifted a little at the front, and she turned to do exactly that, but a moment later her wrist was yet again imprisoned by another equally strong grip, and she was being drawn away from the party.

'Hey,' she muttered, but Alejandro didn't let go until they were on the fringes of the guests, and then he drew her even further away, towards the river once more.

'You do *not* look like you've been drawn backwards through a bush,' he said with barely controlled anger. 'Instead, you look like a woman who's been thoroughly ravished and, God help me, I want to finish what we started.'

Sienna's lips fell apart. She gaped at him, in what she was sure was her least Olivia look yet. She scrambled for something to say. 'You stopped what we were doing,' was about as clever as she could manage.

'Yes.' He put his hands on his hips, staring at her, a muscle pulsing in the base of his jaw. 'Does she often speak to you like that?'

Sienna's cheeks paled. 'Forget about it.'

He moved closer and she trembled, her emotions overwrought, her body incapable of doing anything but responding to his nearness.

'But she's right. I should go and make myself presentable.'

'You are *very* presentable.' He took a step closer.

'What are you doing?'

'I don't know.' He stared at her, complex emotions darkening his eyes to a stormy grey.

'A minute ago you didn't want me—'

He pressed a finger to her lips and her eyes shut in instinctive response. The contact felt insanely good…

'You cannot truly believe that?'

'I might not be as experienced as you, Alejandro—' heaven help her, but the taste of his name in her mouth was incredibly erotic; she rolled each syllable over her tongue, delighting in the feel of it '—but that doesn't mean I don't recognise a lack of enthusiasm.'

His laugh was a short, sharp sound, rich with disbelief. 'You recognise nothing.'

She looked away, not in the mood to be lied to, flattered. She'd mistaken what they were doing, what he'd felt. She'd embarrassed herself by basically throwing herself at him…

'My experience is partly why I stopped,' he ground out, dropping his hand from her mouth. But instead of withdrawing it from her completely, he let it fall to her hip, gripping her close.

Sienna was holding on to her pride by a thread. She wanted to understand *why* but didn't dare ask. She didn't want to do anything to reveal how much she cared.

'You are nothing like the women I usually take to bed.'

Her pulse ratcheted up a gear. 'There's no bed here.'

'Fine. Have sex with.'

The raw description of what they'd been doing set her blood well and truly on fire.

'I can imagine the myriad ways in which I'm different.'

He frowned. 'I mean that you are sheltered. Innocent.'

Her mouth formed a circle of surprise.

'You are not experienced, and I refuse to take advantage of you. Not when, for me, it would just be—' He paused, searching for the words.

'Another notch on your bedpost?'

He lifted a darkly sculpted brow, not rejecting the claim. 'More or less.'

Her heart kerthunked against her ribs. So it wouldn't mean anything to him. He wasn't offering more than this—just one night. A night in Rome, beneath the stars, him, her and sex, finally, so she could at least be assured that she wouldn't end up getting married while she was still a virgin. And she *must* get married, at some point in the next twenty months—the time was drawing closer, and in the back of her mind she had been panicking about the idea of walking down the aisle while still so inexperienced. She didn't mind marrying someone she barely knew and didn't desire, but she resented, a lot, the necessity of doing so without having gained some experience first. Didn't she deserve this?

'So you *did* want to sleep with me?'

'Sleep had absolutely nothing to do with what I wanted,' he responded with a mocking glint in his eyes.

She pushed aside his attempt at humour. There was too much at stake. Suddenly, Sienna was envisaging having her cake and eating it too and she suspected it would be rather delicious.

'What you *wanted*?' She lifted her hand to his chest, her fingers splayed wide as she felt the steady, heavy thundering of his heart beneath her palm. 'Or what you *want*?'

He stared down at her, looking almost as though he were in physical pain. Why was he fighting this? She was torn between her rational, thinking brain and the part of her that had been filled, her entire life, with the worst kind of insults from her mother that made it easy to believe he could never be attracted to her—even when her brain assured her that he was. But she could have sworn he desired her. So why wouldn't he act on it? What was it that was holding him back? It was as if an invisible barrier had formed between them and she wanted, more than anything, to push through it.

'Drop it.' The words were harsh. She blinked in surprise and he winced. 'I'm sorry. But you have to understand—'

Impatience ignited in her gut. 'What? What do I have to understand?' She put her hands on her hips, so frustrated she could barely breathe. She was frustrated by her mother and the cruel taunts she'd lived with for so long, with the limitations that had been put on her life by her father's cruel will, but mostly she was frustrated by the man in front of her, who was saying one thing with his body and another with his words.

'You are a very beautiful woman—'

She made an exasperated sound. 'I don't need to be told I'm beautiful.'

'But this isn't going to happen.'

She narrowed her eyes. 'What if I want to be a notch on your bedpost?'

He stared at her, that same tortured expression on his face. 'You don't.'

'How do you know?'

'Sienna—'

The warning note in his voice tipped her over. Irritated and impatient, she lifted a finger to his lips. 'I'm going to kiss you. If you really don't want this to go any further, walk away right now. Otherwise, stop making excuses and give us what we both want.'

'You want—'

'To be treated like a consenting adult, capable of making up my own mind about what I do and don't want. If *you* don't want *me*, then have the guts to say as much.'

Surprise showed in his face and she waited—somehow—for three seconds, before she reached up and put a hand to the back of his head, drawing him closer. When they kissed, it was like the bursting of a dam wall; passion threatened to drown them both, and relief was a flood inside Sienna's chest. She *knew* she'd been right.

'Come with me.' She laced her fingers through his and pulled before either of them could give this a second thought.

CHAPTER THREE

HE KNEW ENOUGH to know he should put a stop to this, that his friendship with Luca demanded that, so why did he follow her? Why didn't he say something?

'Sienna—'

'No.' She turned to face him, her eyes scanning his face. 'This is happening, Alejandro. I know I'm not as experienced as you, but I know enough to be able to tell when someone's attracted to me.'

'Attracted? Undoubtedly.' She waited, and the word 'but' hovered on his lips, yet he didn't utter it. And suddenly, he was a teenager again, having to make decisions of which he wasn't proud, to go against his own code of morals simply to survive. But having sex with Sienna wasn't a question of survival. So why did it feel as though it were?

Sienna didn't know how she stayed standing upright when every single bone in her body seemed to be trembling. She pushed the door to the room inwards, ignoring the fussy, froufrou décor, ignoring everything but the way his hand felt wrapped around hers, the way her heart was thumping solidly and excitely for the first time in her life that she was finally taking her destiny into her own hands and claiming what *she* wanted, because *she* wanted it, not for anyone else. She was abandoning her virginity when it suited *her*, not because her father had dictated from beyond the grave that she would need to marry, not because her groom would expect sex to be a component of their marriage. This was her choice, her terms, her life! The rush of power she felt was an added aphrodisiac and she revelled in its delightful possession of her body.

As soon as the door clicked shut he was kissing her again, but without restraint—not that she could have said he was restrained before, but this was different, his mouth taking over her soul completely, the weight of his body pushing her backwards, until they connected with the elegant rococo chaise longue across the room. Neither reached for the lights, so the room was barely illuminated, and Sienna was glad—it heightened her other senses, not being able to see, plus it removed any need for self-consciousness.

She had barely fallen back onto the chaise longue before his hands were pushing at her dress, desperation removing any lingering doubt from her mind that he wanted this as much as she did, that the chemistry she felt wasn't one-sided.

But when his fingers brushed the simple white cotton of her briefs, she froze, embarrassed, even in the midst of passion, at the utilitarian nature of her underwear. She had no doubt what kind of frothy, lacy situation his lovers usually wore.

If he noticed, or cared, he said nothing, simply sliding them down her legs and disposing of them before bringing his mouth back to hers, the weight of his body on her as he kissed her, his tongue flicking her, rolling with hers, and she arched her back in silent, desperate need.

If she'd loved the feel of his name before, she loved it even more now, every time she cried it, passion infusing each syllable, filling her soul with desperate hunger.

'*Cristo,*' he muttered. 'You make me feel as though I am a schoolboy again, making love for the first time.'

His accent was so much thicker, his voice ragged, as he stripped out of his shirt, staring at her with what could have been taken as annoyance. Given his admission just now, she supposed it was, but annoyance with himself? The feeling he'd damaged his pride?

She smiled up at him, the compliment doing something funny to her heart, her chest, her stomach, so she bit down on her lip and he groaned, dropping forward even as his arms still worked to disentangle themselves from the crisp white shirt.

'*La marta...*' he murmured against her lips.

She spoke Spanish fluently—had taught herself as a way to fill in the empty weekends of teenagerdom—so knew that he was calling her a minx. It made her laugh. Where were the nerves she'd expected to feel? Where was the uncertainty?

She felt nothing but a wild, heady rush of gladness and need, and she felt them in a large enough quantity to forget everything else.

'This is heaven.' She pushed his shirt down the rest of the way, lifting her legs up and wrapping them around his waist even as she dropped his shirt to the ground. He rolled his hips and she cried out, because he was *so close*, his arousal pressed right to her most intimate flesh, so it almost felt as though he were already inside her.

'I want to take my time, but I know you have not got long,' he whispered into her ear, but his voice was thick and gravelled when he turned to meet her eyes. 'People will come looking for you.'

No, nobody would look for her. Nobody would care that she was missing. And nobody would expect that she'd be doing this—nor he doing it with her. The deliciousness of that secret bloomed in her chest. She smiled, pushed onto her elbows and kissed him, while at the same time she reached for his pants and unfastened them. This time, he didn't stop her. This time, he let her push them down and moved his legs to finish the job, so seconds later this Spanish deity brought to life was naked on top of her, his bronzed, sculpted body so beautiful to feel; she could only wish it were possible to see all of him too. She wanted to push him to standing and command him to pirouette for her, to allow her time to admire him in the barely there light, but standing would mean distance and she wasn't willing to risk that.

'A moment.' The word was hoarse. Without pulling too far away from her, he reached down, fingers wrapping around his leather wallet, which he dug from the fabric of his pockets, and flicked it open one-handed to remove a condom. Her breath hissed from her lips as she watched him roll it over his length, the darkness meaning she could see only the silhouette of his body, and the length of his arousal froze her to the core. How the hell was that going to fit?

She bit down on her lip, terrified that maybe she

couldn't do this after all, but then he was kissing her again. Had he sensed something had shifted? Did he feel her hesitation?

Of course not. He wasn't a bloody mind-reader. He was just a very experienced lover—so experienced he'd somehow intuited that she was 'innocent'. He was giving her time to relax, that was all.

His hands found the top of her dress, pushing it down over her breasts, and Sienna could have sworn she heard the fabric tear slightly, but it barely registered because the moment the dress was down he was feeling her breasts in his hands, the weight of each in his palms, rolling them, his fingers brushing over her nipples. She'd gone out with a guy once who'd touched her breasts. He'd said they were like cantaloupes—he'd meant it as a compliment but ever since then Sienna had been mortified by her huge breasts and done whatever she could to disguise them—and she'd never been able to eat any kind of melon again, which was a shame because until then cantaloupes had been one of her favourite fruits and had the added benefit of being detested by her mother, so Sienna had snacked on them often, if only to annoy Angelica. After Ryan Hawkins, she'd never touched them again.

But Alejandro's touch wasn't like that. He was gentle and possessive at the same time, making her feel as though he had to touch her breasts in order to be able to survive, making her feel as though this were the beginning and end of his world. She arched her back, and then he took one nipple in his mouth—everything evaporated from her mind in a single, shuddering explosion, until a second later his fingers were between her legs, so she had two parts of her body feeling as though they were bursting into literal flame and she simply couldn't cope, even when she also couldn't bear him to stop.

'This is perfect,' she ground out, rolling her hips in an ancient, feminine invitation for more.

He spoke softly in Spanish and, despite her fluency, her brain was too jam-packed with new sensations and feelings, so that she couldn't translate, she couldn't understand, she knew only that his words made her feel good, like pouring warm, melted caramel over her skin.

'Please,' she groaned as his fingers massaged a cluster of nerve endings that had her whimpering hard. She was the only person who'd ever touched herself there, and never like this. Never so skilfully, so masterfully, never with the same mix of pressure then release, so just as she felt she was about to experience relief, he pulled away. Moist heat pooled between her legs; stars jumped behind her eyes, and, out of nowhere, pain.

Stretching, strange, new pain.

Sharp, searing, so she half sat up and cried out, their eyes locking, his showing, at this proximity, obvious shock, hers confusion, until she realised he'd removed his hand and simply thrust into her, his whole length, all of him, at once, and she hadn't been prepared, even though she had, really, been very skilfully prepared, at the same time.

'What the…?' He swallowed a rough Catalan curse at the end of the sentence—a language in which Sienna knew only the basics. His face showed torment, shock. Anger.

'What—'

'Tell me you were not a virgin.'

Confusion swamped her, and also something else. Something warm and pleasurable, something that was making her blood boil again. Pain was receding, and now pleasure was picking up right where it had left off, so she shook her head, her nails digging into his shoulder as she dragged him downwards. 'Later. We'll talk. But now, please.'

He swore again, this time in Spanish, so she understood it fully, and even if she hadn't the tone of his voice left her in little doubt that he hadn't been expecting this. Except he *had* been. He'd said as much outside.

'Sienna—' The word was a warning, and it was also a plea. For what? Reassurance? She caught his face on either side, holding him still.

'I came in here because I wanted this. Please don't stop. And please don't make me beg. Make love to me, Alejandro.'

'But your first time—' He swore again. 'It shouldn't be with someone like me.' The words were urgent. 'It shouldn't be like this.'

She moved her finger to his lips, pressing it there first, before sliding it into his mouth, removing it, then sliding it into her own mouth. 'I wanted this. I chose you.'

His eyes closed as he emitted a low, throaty groan. 'Oh, for God's sake,' he muttered, pulling out a little, so she held her breath, before he pushed back in, deeper, gently, but also in a way that reminded her he was in charge—as she suspected Alejandro always would be.

Every movement was like the tightening of a coil, the winding of it around and around, so she could barely think, barely breathe, but when he brought his mouth to her breasts once more and suckled on one nipple first, then the next, she was barely able to hold on to sense, and life. She dug her nails into his shoulders hard, then dragged them down his back, so hard she wondered, in the very back of her mind, if she might have drawn blood, before digging them into his buttocks, clinging on as pleasure exploded through her, tipping her over the edge of sanity and self, so all she could do was cry his name, so loudly that he had no option but to kiss her, hard, to swallow the syllables into his mouth as his own climax tormented his body, racking it in waves, until, like a ship wrecked to shore, he collapsed on top of her. He was no longer sure of a damned thing, knowing only that he'd been wrong: regret would not wait until morning.

'Wow. Just…wow.'

Alejandro was still riding the wave, his breath burning inside his chest, his whole body feeling as though it had been zapped by an electrical current, every cell reverberating with completion and contentment, so that he would have liked to lie there for a moment, relishing every last sensation, before rousing them both back to fever pitch again, and again. Despite the force of his orgasm, his body wasn't anywhere near satisfied. He wanted more. He wanted to explore her, to experience her in every way.

Which was a goddamned warning he heeded.

Pulling away from her, he stared down at her innocently flushed face for just long enough to confirm that she was experiencing a sexual awakening, just long enough for guilt and self-recriminations to overtake everything else, so he pushed up completely to standing and turned his back, wishing there were some way to undo what had just happened.

But even as he thought that, he knew himself well enough to doubt—would he really take it back? Chemistry had overwhelmed them both and it had been a long time since Alejandro had been with a woman in such an organic, essential way. Since he'd felt as though he might die if he didn't sleep with someone. He ground his teeth together as he disposed of the condom and reached for his pants, all without looking at her. He couldn't. He was furious—with himself mainly, but also with her, and he knew enough to know it would be reprehensible to castigate her right after taking her virginity. He snapped on the light with force, anger reverberating through him, an anger he knew he shouldn't—couldn't—express to her.

But damn it, she should have told him. He wasn't the kind of man who would take advantage of a woman like this. He wasn't the kind of man to get involved with virgins. All his life, he'd known the importance of proving to himself, with every decision he made, that he was nothing like his father. Nothing like the man who'd seduced an inexperienced, trusting virgin, made her fall in love, then disappeared into thin air when she'd revealed that she'd fallen pregnant. He had never slept with a virgin. Not even close. Until this night, and it was something he would never have chosen for himself. He didn't have a 'type', in terms of looks. Tall, short, brunette, blonde, curvaceous or trim, Alejandro couldn't explain what features he was attracted to, but he knew, beyond a shadow of a doubt, that sexual experience was a prerequisite. He ordinarily slept with women who were as uninterested in relationships as he was. Women who understood the way he worked. Anxiety tightened in his gut, because even without the proof of her virginity he'd known she wasn't like that. Sienna was gentle and sweet, and definitely not used to mixing in the kinds of social circles he did.

Even without this discovery, he'd known this was wrong. Luca. Oh, *mierda*. Luca. Defying Luca had been bad enough when he'd thought Sienna experienced, but knowing what he did now, he understood why Luca had warned Alejandro away. She wasn't suitable to be one of his one-night stands. Luca had been one hundred per cent right.

He groaned softly, then forced himself to face her, anger and disbelief pummelling his body from the inside out. She was still lying there, wonder on her face, cheeks pink, eyes sparkling, her magnificent breasts round and full, revealed to the full hunger of his gaze, dress ruched around her midsection—*Cristo*, he hadn't even taken the time to undress her properly, so great had his hunger been. He'd treated her like any of his usual conquests, like a woman *au fait* with life and sex. He'd treated her like his equal in this regard, and even after knowing her a short time, he recognised that she'd deserved better.

His lips assumed a grim line. 'That is *not* what your first time should have been.'

She tilted her face to the side, eyeing him thoughtfully. 'Do I look as though I'm complaining?'

Despite his regret, pride swelled in his chest. Childish, arrogant pride. He quelled it. He didn't deserve any hint of pride, not after what he'd done. Heat flushed his skin as he felt the full weight of his betrayal. Less than an hour after assuring Luca he'd care for Sienna, he'd taken her virginity in the powder room of a restaurant. Self-directed anger made his voice harsher than he intended. 'You should have told me.'

It seemed to dawn on Sienna that something was wrong. She sat up a little, reaching for the floaty straps of her dress and bending her face forward as she focussed on securing them in place, so his fingertips tingled with a desire to reach out and stop her. He wanted her to stay like this for ever—no, not for ever, he didn't believe in such a concept, but for a little while longer, until he'd committed her spectacular curves to his permanent memory.

She frowned. 'You called me innocent outside. I thought you knew.'

He stared at her, perplexed, before recalling that, yes, he had referred to her in this way. He brushed a hand through the air. 'I meant that you are innocent relative to me, not completely inexperienced. Tell me you do have *some* experience with men?'

She nodded, just once, her lips pressed together so their outline was a soft white.

'You are too old to have been a virgin.' Too old, too beautiful, too sensual, too hypnotic. How was it possible?

Her eyes lifted to his and she stood, uneasily, unsteadily, so he reached out a hand to offer stability but she flinched away, the features of her beautiful face stiff.

'The facts would beg to differ.'

'Fine, you were a virgin, but *how*?'

'Isn't that obvious? I've simply never had sex before.'

Sex wasn't supposed to be special and intimate. It wasn't supposed to be memorable. It was a transaction, brief and satisfying but of the moment. And now, more importantly, he didn't want to remember that for the first time in his life he'd betrayed a man he thought of more as family than a friend.

Heat exploded at the crown of his head as he came face to face with the reality of what he'd done. But she looked at him with those enormous green eyes and he felt a thousand other things too, emotions that were at odds with his way of living, emotions he shut down before they could take hold.

'This was a very regrettable mistake, Sienna. I wish it had never happened.'

Sienna wasn't an idiot. She knew it would have been poor form to spring her virginity on some unsuspecting partner, but he'd called her innocent and he'd been so gentle with her, as if preparing her for the first time a man's body possessed hers. She'd simply got caught up in the moment, without feeling a need to spell out the true reasons she had never let things go this far with a man. But what they'd shared would never be categorised as a mistake for her.

'I'm sorry you feel that way. And don't worry, I'm not hoping for a proposal or anything. You might not have known I was a virgin—and I'm sorry for that, I truly believed you had somehow intuited the truth—but *I* knew. I knew, and I chose to do this. You didn't take advantage of me.' She scanned his face. 'And you were very clear about what we were going to share, so my expectations from twenty minutes ago to now haven't changed.'

'I used you for sex, Sienna. Are you really okay with that?'

The directness of his words delighted her. Sienna much preferred that to being called 'beautiful'.

'And *I* used *you* right back! I've got no problems with what we just did. In fact, my only problem is that it's over, because I really enjoyed it.'

He stared at her, completely gobsmacked. 'You're being deliberately facetious.'

'No, I'm just pointing out the ridiculous hypocrisy of your perspective. I was a virgin, fine, but I'm still a woman in my twenties with more than two brain cells to rub together. I knew what you were offering, and I absolutely knew what I was doing when we walked in here together.' She tilted her chin at him, brave, fierce eyes daring him to disagree.

Intrigue flooded his features. 'And that was having sex for the first time in your life, with a man you just met?

'You should have been honest with me,' he continued.

'Would you have slept with me if you'd known?'

'Absolutely not.'

The speed of his response floored her. She stared at him, gasping for air, shocked and confused.

'Virgin or not, it was a mistake, but your innocence complicates it.'

'I'm sorry—'

'Don't apologise.' Now it was Alejandro who grimaced. 'And I am not entirely sure it is you who owes one.' The cryptic response didn't make sense, but before she could question him he continued. 'It shouldn't have happened, but we cannot change the fact it did.'

'No,' she murmured, grateful then that a lifetime of being torn down by her mother had given her a kick-ass ability in hiding her feelings. 'But we can do the next best thing and just pretend it never happened.'

CHAPTER FOUR

BEFORE LUCA HAD drawn his attention to Sienna, Alejandro had barely noticed her. He'd been brooding, wondering what had happened to change Luca from the man he knew—a man he felt an affinity with in so many ways—to a doting, adoring, puppy-dog-esque husband, all of a sudden.

But now, Sienna was all he was aware of. He watched from a distance as she moved through the party. Hell, he could still smell her on him, taste her, if he closed his eyes he could *feel* her muscles tightening around his hardness, so he didn't close his eyes, he didn't allow himself to sink back into that memory. It wasn't how he operated.

He watched her, a beer in one hand, grateful for the shadows that turned his symmetrical face into a chiaroscuro, obscuring him from notice, thankful that Luca was now too absorbed in his bride to notice anyone or anything else, because Alejandro had no idea how he'd ever be able to meet his friend in the eye again.

Besides, Sienna looked happy.

She looked as though he was the furthest thing from her mind. She'd stopped walking and was now talking to an older woman with short silver hair and a dress that was the brightest shade of pink Alejandro had ever seen.

As he watched, Sienna laughed at something her companion said, her head tilted back, her fabulous red hair like a beacon. He wanted to catch it all in his hand and wrap it around his fist, tilting her head back until her eyes stared into his and her mouth was open, waiting, needing…

He swore. It was time to get out of here, before he did something really stupid and suggested they spend the night together.

And yet he didn't move. He stayed where he was, watching, wondering, wanting.

'You know I'm not ready to settle down, Gertie. Not yet.'

'But all these men!' Gertie gestured to the party, shaking her head. 'So many options.'

'Yes, and none of them right for me.' Sienna followed Gertie's gaze, using all of her willpower to avoid so much as glancing within a dozen metres of Alejandro, even though she knew exactly where he was, even though she could feel his eyes on her in a way that was making her pulse flutter unsteadily.

'What about my Andrew? You know he thinks the world of you.'

Sienna rolled her eyes, an indulgent smile softening her lips. 'I *work* for him. Have you heard of a small matter of sexual harassment?'

'It is not harassment if you agree to date, and he would make you happy.'

'Gertie.' Sienna laughed, shaking her head. 'It's never going to happen.'

Gertie tilted her hot-pink lips. 'That's a shame. I should have liked to claim you as my granddaughter-in-law.'

Sienna softened, putting a hand on the older woman's shoulder. 'How about just keeping me as a friend?'

'And a lawn bowls partner?' Gertie grinned, chinking her champagne flute to Sienna's.

Sienna sipped in agreement, her head tilted back, so she missed the moment they were joined by another.

'Ah, speak of the devil.'

'I thought my ears were burning.' Andrew Davison—the Earl of Highbury, and also Sienna's boss—approached, holding two champagne flutes. 'Actually, I thought you could both use a drink, but I see you've got that covered.'

Andrew was one of the few people who understood a little of what Sienna's life was like—courtesy of her close friendship with Gertie, cemented when Sienna was only a teenager, and she had been truly miserable, and now their own friendship. He knew that while Sienna was very happy for her sister's marriage, any family event brought with it a tension for Sienna that was almost off the Richter scale.

'That doesn't mean a second drink wouldn't be welcome.' Sienna smiled through gritted teeth, wishing that her entire body didn't feel *different*. Her nipples were so sensitive that every movement brought the fabric of her dress brushing over them, making goosebumps dance on her pale skin, and between her legs there was a throbbing that made it impossible to forget Alejandro, that made it impossible not to want him again.

But that would never happen.

He'd made it clear that he wished they'd never slept together, and she wasn't going to debase herself by begging.

'No man is ever going to want a fat slob like you, Sienna. What did I do to deserve you as a daughter? Tell me that.'

She finished one glass of champagne, then took the other from Andrew. Kindly concern shaped his eyes so she smiled, a practised smile of reassurance, as she took the glass from him.

Gertie wasn't wrong. Her grandson was gorgeous. Definitely eligible bachelor material—strange that Sienna had never so much as looked at him in that light. Oh, he was perhaps too old for her, in his mid-thirties, but then, how old was Alejandro? What was his last name? She gasped, shocked by how little she knew of a man who knew every detail about her body, covering the surprised reaction by quickly drinking from the champagne. That was what they'd agreed after all. Just sex. No strings. No promises. And she was fine with that. No regrets.

'My driver is out the front. You know you are welcome to use his services to escape at any time,' Andrew said, leaning closer, so only she heard the offer.

He thought she was upset about the wedding, and about her mother. He couldn't know that a whole other incident had usurped everything else in her mind.

'Thank you, but I have to stay until Olivia leaves. It will raise questions if I ghost earlier.'

'Fair enough. But the offer is there.'

'Lord Highbury.' She would know Alejandro's voice anywhere. She stiffened, turning to face him, wondering how long he'd been standing there.

'Alex!' To her surprise, mild-mannered Andrew smiled broadly, reaching out an enthusiastic hand and shaking Alejandro's—Alex's—in it. 'I didn't know you'd be here.'

'Luca and I went to school together.' He flicked his gaze to Sienna and a thousand sparks ignited. There was anger simmering in his gaze. Or was she misreading him? She couldn't say. Her fingers curled more tightly around her champagne.

'Of course, of course. I should have thought. I haven't seen you in almost a year. Are you well?'

How did Andrew know Alejandro? And how well?

'Yes.' He didn't ask the same questions of Andrew. 'I promised Sienna a dance earlier. Excuse me.' He reached for her hand and she was so surprised that she didn't pull away, she didn't say anything, she simply stared up at him, the contact searing her soul.

'And who are you?' Gertie's voice, though made frail by age, still reached through the tension, drawing Alejandro's impatient gaze.

'Alejandro Corderó.'

Corderó. She tasted the word in her mouth, whispering it to herself, before realising that Gertie was watching her from between shrewd eyes.

Pull it together.

'And how do you know our Sienna?'

The possessive nature of the question was obvious, so too his reaction: his hand tightening around hers.

'Through Luca. Excuse us.'

Belatedly, as they cut through the crowd, Sienna went to pull her hand away but he held it fast, his eyes turning to her, pinning her with a warning.

'What are you doing?' she muttered.

'Dancing.'

'I don't want to dance with you,' she lied, and he knew it was a lie, a look of mockery on his face when he turned to face her. He didn't take her to the middle of the dance floor and she was glad; instead, he found a spot on the edge, where there was less light, more privacy, and pulled her into his arms, holding her against his chest.

Sparks flew. She felt each and every one of them embed in her body, felt their heat and warmth, and knew the answer to that warmth, she knew exactly how to relieve them. 'I am leaving after this dance.'

Emptiness trapped her stomach. She stopped moving, and simply stared up at him. It was a betraying gesture and she hated herself for showing it to him, but it occurred to Sienna that she was never going to see this man again. She hadn't expected she would, and yet the realisation that he was about to walk out of her life just as abruptly as he'd walked into it filled her mouth with sawdust.

'Fine. It's late. I'm sure Luca won't mind. I need to stay until the end, until my sister leaves—'

She was babbling. She clamped her lips together and focussed on a point to the right of his shoulder. He drew her closer, holding her body against his body, so she was aware of every part of him, aware of what he felt like, of what he looked like, aware of how his weight had pressed her to the chair, aware of what it was to want someone with your whole, entire heart. Except her heart wasn't the issue, so much as a suddenly awakened libido.

'Listen to me.'

She swallowed, pressing her lips together, waiting.

'I presumed you were experienced. Not necessarily very experienced, but that you at least had some.'

She glared at him. 'Sorry to disappoint you.'

His eyes flashed to hers. 'I did not say I was disappointed by *anything* we shared, *querida*.'

And despite the grim look on his face, she felt a hum of warmth at the admission—or as close as he was going to get to an actual admission—that he had enjoyed what they'd shared *despite* her inexperience.

'I presume you are not on the pill?'

Her eyes widened. She shook her head slowly, feeling like a complete idiot for not having thought of that.

'I see.'

'But you used protection, so there's nothing to worry about, right?'

'Condoms are not one hundred per cent effective. There is a possibility that you have conceived my child.'

She dropped her hands to her sides, the idea exploding in her mind, so she shook her head without even thinking it through.

'That can't be—'

'Of course it can be.' His voice was without emotion, and yet she felt it emanating off him in waves. 'I would expect you to contact me if there are any consequences from what we just shared.'

'There won't be,' she said, because it had to be true. She had never thought about becoming a parent. It wasn't something she'd ever craved, and it certainly wasn't on her agenda any time soon.

'You will let me know either way.'

She swallowed past a heaviness that had built in her throat. 'I'll let you know if there's anything to know,' she conceded. 'Of course.'

Silence fell. He stared at her as though he were trying to read her mind and a moment later, a grim tone to his voice, he asked, 'Did I hurt you?'

She blinked, not understanding at first. 'When?'

'I was not gentle. Not like I would have been, if I'd known—'

'Oh.' She pulled her lower lip between her teeth. 'No. I'm—fine.'

But she could see guilt about the corners of his eyes and wanted to alleviate it better.

'I don't know if I'm meant to say this, because, you know, I have no experience, obviously, but I actually really liked that you weren't gentle. I liked…' She pulled her lips to the side, wondering if she was admitting too much to him. She shook her head. 'I'm fine.'

He expelled a slow breath, as though he was relaxing, but for Sienna the panic was just setting in. Olivia worried about her so much, if Sienna were to have fallen pregnant poor Olivia would probably insist on moving home to England, just to help. If she thought there was even the slightest chance, Olivia would swing into full-blown protective-older-sister mode.

'Listen to me.' Sienna lifted her hand to his chest,

pressing it there with urgency. 'No one can know about what we did.'

His eyes narrowed, darkening. 'I am not in the habit of sharing my exploits with other people, Sienna. My opinion is that private lives should remain exactly that—private. I wasn't intending to discuss what we shared with anyone.' But there was a tone to his voice, as though he was torn about something, as though he was unsure.

'Good.' She was, momentarily, placated. 'As far as I'm concerned, what happened between us was about you and me and nobody else. No one needs to know. Especially not my sister or Luca. They'd completely flip out and they've got enough going on in their own lives without having to worry about mine.'

'I will tell nobody.'

He dropped his arms, taking a step away from her, then reaching into his wallet and removing a black business card. 'But do not forget, Sienna. You'll call me if there is any news to deliver.'

She took the card, stared at the number and, when she looked up, Alejandro had turned his back and was walking away, disappearing into the balmy night air.

Eight dates after leaving Rome, Alejandro had to admit two things to himself: he was bored out of his brain, and he wanted to see Sienna again. To be fair, it hadn't taken him eight dates with eight separate women to realise he was trying to replace rich red wine with tepid water, but he was stubborn, and thinking about Sienna seemed particularly stupid, given that Luca was his best friend and he would definitely *not* approve of the

X-rated direction of Alejandro's thoughts. And yet, here he was, disappointing yet another old flame by not inviting her home with him, knowing that bedding another woman wouldn't work.

He didn't want to have sex with just anyone.

He wanted more of Sienna. He wanted to explore her properly. To taste her. To tease her. To watch her in the full light as she came apart at the seams. He wanted to make her explode, one passionate caress after another, until he was the only person who could put her back together again. He wanted to let their chemistry burn hot, until it had finally burned out, and then he wanted to walk away, just as he had this time. But it had been premature. He'd made a mistake.

Was it one he could fix?

He strode into his penthouse, through the large open space with double-height ceilings, his eyes travelling the details of the skyline visible from the floor-to-ceiling windows and wrap-around terrace. The ornate, recognisable roofs of the Passeig de Gràcia stood in the foreground and, beyond them, Barcelona glittered like an overflowing jewellery box. He paused just long enough to grab a beer from the fridge and kick off his shoes, then he swung open the glass doors to the terrace, stepping out with a grim expression on his handsome face.

Eight days.

That was barely any time. A blip. He knew from experience that all things became easier with time's passage. He simply had to go through the motions a little longer, and eventually he'd cease to think of her, eventually he would no longer want her. He had no choice: wanting her was forbidden.

* * *

'Here, Starbuck, here.' She rubbed behind her dog's ears, the big, open-mouthed, slobbery smile she got in return making Sienna laugh. She crouched down, pressing her chin to Starbuck's head. 'You really are a one-off, girl.'

She pulled back a little, but Starbuck only plonked her furry body down onto the flagstones, resting her own chin on Sienna's legs.

'I see. Are we taking a nap now?'

Starbuck breathed out heavily in response.

Sienna stroked the hair between Starbuck's ears, distracted, happy to rest a moment, to stare out of the open double doors into the almond grove she could just make out directly ahead of her. How many hours had she and Olivia spent hiding out there, away from their parents, pretending they were pirates on the open seas, far away from Hughenwood House and the horrors of their parents' marriage?

She closed her eyes, pushing away those unpleasant memories, and landing right in far more pleasant ones. His hands on her body. His mouth at her breasts. His fiery Spanish words in her ears, working their way into her heart. She groaned and Starbuck shifted, casting a lazy look up before returning to her resting place.

It had been three weeks since the wedding. Three weeks since she'd met Alejandro Corderó and suffered a temporary bout of insanity that had seen her throw herself at the man, regardless of her lack of experience.

It was tempting—and easy—to blame her mother, who'd spent the entire morning of the wedding nitpicking Sienna until she was ready to blow a gasket—

she just hadn't known she wanted to blow that particular one! But Angelica Thornton-Rose had been on Sienna's case her entire life. Why had that day been any different? Why hadn't she been able to fend off her mother's attacks as always, filing them away into the 'bitter, vain, aging widow' category of her mind?

Because it hadn't really been about Angelica. It had been about Alejandro. All about him, and his unique impact on her. She'd wanted him and, as was often the case with Sienna, she'd acted on her impulses. She hadn't stopped to question the wisdom of sleeping with her brother-in-law's best friend. She hadn't stopped to question *anything*. She'd wanted him and so she'd done whatever she could to have him, to hell with the consequences.

And yet, there were none. Three weeks later, she'd had confirmation she wasn't pregnant and, as further evidence of insanity, had actually felt a blip of disappointment and emptiness to realise there was no reason to call him. Imagine that! Tethering herself to a man like him for all eternity simply because he'd made her body feel something she'd never known possible.

No amount of orgasms could make sharing a child with Alejandro worth it. Right?

She bit down on her lip, wishing she were fully convinced of that, and for the hundredth time since the wedding she pulled out her phone and loaded up his number. She'd saved it into the phone that night, discarding his business card. She'd known she'd lose it anyway—Sienna was about as organised as the Mad Hatter after a barrel of wine when it came to paperwork. She stared at the screen, wondering what it would be like to press that little green button. To hear his voice. Just his voice.

She stared at her phone and the impulse to do exactly that was so strong her fingertip actually felt as though it were fizzing. Extricating herself from serving as Starbuck's pillow, she stood up and paced towards the door, her heart racing as hard and fast as if she were back at the wedding, Alejandro right in front of her.

What have you got to lose?

How about your pride? a stubborn voice reminded her.

After all, a lifetime of being told she was no good couldn't help but shape the way in which she viewed herself, even when Olivia had done her level best to push Angelica's cruelty aside as though it meant nothing. And weren't some things worth a gamble? Look at Olivia! She'd risked everything by going to Rome and asking Luca to marry her.

Sienna didn't want to marry Alejandro, but she wasn't sure it was doing any good to continue pretending she didn't want *something* from him. But would he feel the same way?

There was only one way to know for sure.

CHAPTER FIVE

'SORRY TO INTERRUPT, ALEJANDRO.'

His assistant Maria's voice was clipped and efficient as always. He paused, midway through changing out of his suit and into running gear, clicking the desk phone into speaker mode.

'*Si?*'

He unbuttoned his shirt and discarded it over the back of his chair.

'There's a woman here to see you.'

Bored impatience settled in his gut. 'I'm heading out.'

'I'm aware of the time.' Maria's response brought a tight smile to his lips. They'd worked together six years—other than Luca, she was the person who knew him best in the world.

'I don't take unsolicited appointments.'

'Again, I am aware of how you operate.'

'Then why are you putting through this call?'

He heard Maria sigh and let out a silent laugh. They badgered one another like this for sport.

He stepped out of his trousers, casting them over the back of the seat before reaching for his shorts.

'She says it's important.'

He arched a brow. 'Who, exactly?'

'Sienna Thor—'

He reached for the phone, snapping it out of the cradle before his assistant had finished speaking Sienna's full name.

'She's here?'

His gut twisted as his future suddenly changed shape, and he imagined the sole reason she could have for showing up in his office like this.

She was pregnant.

'Shall I ask her to make an appointment?'

Ashen, he stared at the wall. Alejandro had known two things about himself for as long as he could remember. He would never be a man who lied to women, who promised them more than he wanted to give. And he would never be a man who turned his back on responsibilities. Not as his own father had. If Sienna had conceived as a result of their one time together, then there was nothing for it. They would marry. And Luca would never speak to him again. That would be a grave price in his life, but one he would pay in a heartbeat if the alternative was shirking his paternal duty.

'No. Send her in. *Immediatament.*'

He clicked the phone back into place, not taking his eyes off the wall opposite. His office, a space that was familiar to him by virtue of the fact he spent long, long hours here each day, and had done for years, changed into a different and unfamiliar shape. The whole world looked different. Everything seemed to grind to a halt. He turned to face the door, a ringing in his ears, as he prepared for all the ways in which his life was about to change.

Which meant he spent precisely zero time preparing for the fact Sienna—the object of some seriously dirty dreams of Alejandro's—was about to walk into his office.

But when she did, it was like being shocked with high-voltage electricity.

The colours that had seeped away from his walls were suddenly back, brighter almost than he could bear. As she walked, everything seemed to shimmer. What was it about her that radiated warmth? She was her own source of energy. Her red hair had been swept up into a loose, chaotic bun, and despite the untidiness all he really noticed was the way it drew attention to her cheekbones, her freckles, and those enormous green eyes, her pouting lips begging…

But, no.

That wasn't why she was here, and it sure as hell wasn't a thought process he could engage in, for a thousand reasons.

'Sienna.' He tried to keep his voice businesslike, and he maintained distance between them, because he needed that.

Only, it didn't help. Not when her eyes ravished his face before sinking to his chest, staring at him as though she'd never seen a naked man before. And hell, perhaps she hadn't. Alejandro hadn't got as far as removing his shirt the night they'd made love. A perverse fascination made him want to stay like this, to welcome her inspection, but an awareness of how badly he'd stuffed up at Luca's wedding had dogged him ever since.

Having sinfully wicked dreams about her was one thing, but inviting her to stare at him, wishing she'd touch him, quite another.

And if she was pregnant? And she must be—why else would she be here?

'Please, take a seat.' He gestured to the white leather armchairs arranged by the full floor-to-ceiling windows.

Sienna turned to face the windows, and her distraction allowed him a brief moment of weakness, to allow his own gaze to drift over her body. It was stupid. A foolish move. How could he see her in that summery mini dress and *not* want to rip it off her? She lifted a brown leather backpack from her shoulder, placing it by the door.

He propped his butt on the edge of his desk, a study in nonchalance, as she moved towards the armchairs. She stood behind one, not sitting down, her eyes troubled when they met his.

'Would you like a drink?'

'No, thank you.'

He crossed his arms, watching, waiting, wondering at the hammering of his blood, the throbbing of his central nervous system. He knew the executioner's blade was about to drop, yet even that couldn't stop him from looking at her and wanting a rehash of the last time they'd been alone in the same room together...

But there were bigger, more important issues at play now. He pushed aside his libido with difficulty. 'So I take it we're having a baby together?'

She looked at him as though he'd started speaking Cantonese, and then her cheeks flushed as pink as her beautiful full lips. 'Oh, no.' She shook her head and a clip of her hair dislodged, dropping down beside her cheek. 'I'm not—that's—not why I'm here.'

He didn't visibly react but, inside, emotions were pulling at him, confusing him.

'You said you'd contact me if we had conceived a baby.'

'But we didn't, so I didn't.'

'To be clear, you are not pregnant?'

'No. Definitely not.'

'That's not why you are here?'

'No.'

Relief was a drug. He closed his eyes, pinching the bridge of his nose, as he allowed himself to walk back from the ledge, to return to the vision of his life as he currently knew it. 'Thank *Cristo*.'

When he opened his eyes, it was to find her staring at him, and he realised he still hadn't pulled on a shirt. 'Then what are you doing here?' Dangerous, full-blown temptation simmered in his blood.

Think of Luca.

He'd made the man a promise, and he'd already broken it once. That had been a truly unforgivable mistake, albeit spontaneous. Twice would be a willing, premeditated betrayal.

'Maybe I will take a drink after all.'

'What would you like?'

'Scotch?' she said with a half-smile.

He strode to his liquor cabinet, concealed behind a darkly wooded pantry, and removed a bottle of aged whisky, pouring a measure into a crystal glass, which he carried across the carpeted floor to her.

He could have handed it to her from a safe distance away, but a compulsion he didn't know how to ignore was flooding him. He came around the chair, so they were almost touching, and held it at her chest level. Her fingers reached out to take the glass, wrapping around his, and a thousand electric shocks danced beneath his skin at the simple contact. He dropped his hand away but stayed right where he was.

She let the drink touch her lips at first, and then threw it back in one measure, screwing up her face as the taste assaulted her body. 'That's better.' She coughed a little.

'Water?'

'No, I'm okay.' She kept the glass cradled between both hands, holding it in front of her, so if he leaned forward his chest would brush her hands. 'I just feel a bit ridiculous, being way out on this ledge over here.'

'You're on a ledge?'

'Oh, yeah. A big one.'

'And you wish you weren't?'

'On the contrary, I'm kind of excited.'

'Are you?'

She nodded. He watched, fascinated, as her hair shifted, then dropped his gaze to her breasts. They were truly stunning. His pants strained.

'Yeah. I think so.'

Sensual heat was throbbing through him but there was amusement too. She was unlike any woman he'd ever known, so artless, but charming, and incredibly likeable. Alarm bells sounded in the back of his brain, and he heeded them. He didn't do 'likeable'. It was the nice girls who would get hurt the worst by men like him.

He wasn't going to risk it. Not with Sienna, and not because Luca had warned him off, but because he'd seen what had happened to his mother, how she'd been the quintessential nice girl, too trusting, too innocent, and she'd been completely destroyed by his father.

'Why don't you tell me why you came here?'

She lifted one hand from the glass, tucking that stray clump of hair behind her ear. The action was enough to release a hit of her fragrance—hair conditioner, perfume, hormones—reminding him, powerfully, of the night they'd shared. He was conscious of his body tightening, his arousal starting to strain against the flimsy material of his sports shorts.

'Why aren't you wearing a shirt?'

He'd forgotten about that. 'I was getting ready to go for a run.'

'Oh.' She nodded, but there was a distracted expression on her face. 'Firstly, I've been thinking. And I guess I owe you an explanation after all.'

He stared at her blankly.

'You didn't know I was a virgin.' She darted her tongue out, licking her lower lip. Was she trying to give him a stroke? 'And I didn't know who you were that night, besides being a friend of Luca's—'

Luca. Cristo. *Your best friend.*

'But I do now. I looked you up online. I get what you were saying to me. That whole "notch on the bedpost" thing is no joke with you.'

Why did he wish, more than anything, that he could deny it? Why did he want to tell her that, in fact, he hadn't slept with anyone since her—his longest bout of celibacy since he'd first discovered the wonders of sex.

'Sex seems to be a bit like a sport with you.'

He couldn't help it. He laughed, but at her look of pique he silenced himself, nodding encouragingly. 'Go on.'

'Sex is meaningless for you. That's why you reacted so badly when you realised I was a virgin, because you thought losing my virginity to you would equate to the sex meaning more to me than you wanted it to. Right?'

He didn't deny it. After all, that had been part of it, but what he couldn't confess to her was that Luca had forbidden him from pursuing Sienna, a detail that had weighed on his mind equally.

'But it didn't,' she rushed to reassure him. 'I liked having sex with you, but that's all it was for me as well. The dreams I've been having about you are not about your mind, believe me.'

Another laugh, short and sharp. He resisted asking what the dreams entailed—but only just.

'The thing is, I want to have sex again. With you.'

It was the *last* thing he'd been expecting, and the response was immediate. His body jerked to attention, his mouth went dry, his heart began to thump hard against his ribs, and he had to count to ten just to stop himself from pulling her to the floor here and now.

'Actually, I think I kind of *need* to have sex with you, so that I can stop thinking about it and get on with my life,' she said with a hint of resentment.

It was a living nightmare. A cruel and unusual punishment. That this woman would step into his office and offer herself to him on a platter, when he had sworn to his friend that nothing would happen between them. He couldn't do this. But hell, how he wanted to.

'It's not possible.'

Her eyes dropped to the floor, shielding her emotions from him.

Tell her. Tell her you made a promise to Luca. Tell her you want to screw her more than life itself, but honour and loyalty prevent that from being possible. Tell her this isn't about her, that it's you.

'I see. I thought that might be the case. I mean, you have sex all the time, you probably barely even remember me, but for me, you're just—I mean—I guess I have no clue about it. Is it always like that?'

This was going from bad to worse. If the conversation devolved into talking about the finer points of that night he would forget his own name, let alone Luca's.

'There are other men, more suitable men, to gain experience with.'

She narrowed her eyes suspiciously. 'More suitable how?'

'More inclined to relationships, for one.'

'But that's just it.' Her eyes flashed to his. 'I don't want a relationship. That's not what I'm suggesting.'

His gut tightened. 'You make no sense.'

'Why? You think it's so impossible that a woman should want to live like you do? Okay, not quite like you do, but to have a physical relationship without making a commitment?'

'No. But I don't think that's who *you* are.'

She didn't fight him on that point. 'You don't get it. For reasons that are too complex to go into, I have to get married before I turn twenty-five, which is in a little over a year.'

She was so young. Even without all the other issues,

her age was something he should have paid more attention to. The women he usually went for were closer in age to him—thirty, at least. Uneasiness spread through him.

'You know my feelings on marriage?'

'Yes. I'm not suggesting *we* get married.' She paled visibly, the idea clearly appalling to her. He wondered at that, almost wanted to fight against it on principle—ego, he presumed. 'I need to marry someone, and it would be better if it's not someone I fancy. That would complicate things. I want a husband I can be friends with, but nothing more.'

He stared at her as though she'd sprouted a second head, and then a third.

'As I said, it's complicated.' She waved a hand through the air. 'But before I get married, I want to…' She paused, looking away from him for a moment, then forcing her eyes back to his defiantly. 'I want to know everything I can about sex. To experience it fully.'

'Absolutely not.' He issued the denial swiftly, before he could forget common sense, his obligations to Luca, and every damned reason he had to resist this, and pull her into his arms.

She opened her mouth to protest and then closed it again. Her eyes held his, but there was the smallest slump in her shoulders that made his chest feel hollowed out. A protective instinct he hadn't known in a long time, but that he now realised Sienna invoked, oh, so easily whipped through him. 'Okay, fair enough. I guess it was worth a shot.' She forced a small smile to her face and then skirted around him—far around him—before placing her empty glass on the corner of his desk. She stared at it for several seconds, then slowly pirouetted back towards him. 'Please keep my request between us. I still haven't mentioned anything to Olivia—I don't want her to know any of this.'

He watched her walk towards his door, her back straight, her shoulders squared, and he counted each of his steps, aware that within seconds she'd be gone, out of his life, that the risk would be over. He should have been relieved. He needed this temptation like a hole in the head. But as she approached the door, he felt a surge of adrenaline, a rush of panic, and he knew, even then, that he was losing this fight, and that scared the hell out of him.

'Sienna, wait. Let me explain.' His voice was low and kind, so her heart splintered into a thousand and one pieces. What a fool she'd been! As if he could *ever* feel the same way about her as she did him! Sexual infatuation had gripped her for a long month, tormenting her, but Alejandro Corderó was no stranger to that unique pleasure. He'd had a lot of lovers, if the internet was to be believed. He was hardly pining away for her, wondering about her, waiting for her to swing by his office and ask him to make love to her. How utterly excruciating.

It is a good thing you are smart, Sienna. Your looks are certainly not going to be your success.

'There's no need.' She was as grateful as anything when she reached the door, curving her fingers around the handle. 'I understand.'

'No, you don't.'

'You regretted sleeping with me. Despite my inexperience, that much was obvious.'

His eyes flashed with hers, anger obvious, sparks flecking from him to her and then he was cutting across the office, making short work of the distance, his broad frame right in front of hers so she felt waves of desire and heat buffet her from all sides.

'This is not a question of whether or not I want to sleep with you again. I do.'

She rolled her eyes. 'Please. Don't feel the need to let me down gently. I would always prefer honesty.'

'As would I.' He caught her chin and tilted her face up, so her body jolted with the sheer pressure of awareness. 'So I am being honest with you. This is complicated, not least because of our connection through Luca and Olivia.'

'What difference does that make?'

He stared down at her, his eyes probing hers, reading her, his lips parted, his body tense, and she moaned softly, because this was impossible.

'Look, Alejandro, just forget I came here. You're right. There are other guys I can approach, other men who'll—'

It was as if something snapped inside him. His nostrils flared and then a second later he was right in front of her, temper barely contained. 'Other men? You dare come in here and talk to me about other men—'

'You're the one who said there'd be someone more suitable—'

'I was wrong.' And then he was kissing her, but not as she'd ever been kissed before.

This was a kiss of white-hot possession, a kiss designed to mark her, to change her, and ultimately to claim her. She shivered into his embrace, into the hoarse, Catalan words he groaned into her mouth and she surrendered to him even as she felt a thrill of pleasure, because beyond surrender was the thrill of victory and she let it claim her soul, piece by delicious piece.

CHAPTER SIX

ALEJANDRO EXERCISED CONTROL in all aspects of his life but there was no room for control here, no room for anything but instinct. He'd told her she should find someone else to further her sexual education with and he'd known it was the last thing he wanted, but when she'd thrown that back at him, he'd had to act. Because regardless of what he'd promised Luca, regardless of the limitations of what he could offer Sienna, he wasn't about to let her walk out of his office and into another man's bed.

He couldn't.

Impulses ruled him, just as they had that first night. Impulses that drove thought, reason, obligation and loyalty to Luca from his mind completely, so all he could think about was Sienna and this, and how badly he needed her. He lifted her dress from her head with urgency, dropping it to the floor beside them, not willing to make the same mistake he had last time, leaving her dressed, so that he was unable to appreciate her body properly. It had been dark then too, whereas now the afternoon sun flooded through the mirrored high-rise windows of his office. He wanted to look but that would

mean stepping back, so instead he compromised—
feeling his way over her body, feeling every curve and
undulation, familiarising himself with her sweet spots,
those parts of her that trembled when he touched them,
kissing her as his hands stroked and pulled and plea-
sured, until she was a quivering mess against the door.
He wanted her. He ached for her.

He lifted her as though she weighed nothing, wrapping her legs around his waist as he strode to his desk
and cleared it with one arm, papers landing all over the
floor; he didn't care. He placed her butt on the edge of
his desk and stood between her legs, kissing her more
slowly now as he tried to calm his flaming erection, to
tell himself there was time—or risk coming as soon as
he drove into her.

'Stay here,' he commanded against her mouth, pushing a desk drawer open to reveal a string of condoms.
He lifted one and opened it, rolling it over his length
before meeting her eyes and finding a question there.

'You do this a lot.'

He frowned.

'In your office, I mean.'

'No,' he growled, wondering why it felt important
to clarify that. 'Never.'

He didn't wait to see her response. He'd given her a
straight answer, and now, sheathed and protected from
unwanted consequences, he wanted her more than he
could express.

'Tell me if I hurt you,' he said into her ear.

'You won't.'

'I wasn't gentle enough with you last time. If I had
known—'

'I don't want gentle.' She pressed a hand to his naked chest, her fingertips just touching one of his scars, which ran from one nipple and diagonally downwards. 'I want real.'

'Real? Real I can do.'

And instincts and impulses took over again, so he drew her right to the edge of the desk and drove into her, hard, his first thrust a stake of ownership, a claim on her body that neither had expected, and his next, cementing it. She tilted her head back and his left hand drove through her hair, liberating it from the elastic so it spilled down her back, over her shoulders, her creamy, generous breasts shifting with each movement, her hair brushing them. Desire spiraled into something dangerous, a tornado, as he picked up speed, his fingers moving to her butt, digging into the flesh there as he kept her pushed right to the edge of the desk.

She arched her back instinctively, welcoming him deeper, and he pushed in, her muscles contracting ferociously around his length, until he was simply light and heat, lost to her, this, everything, just as he had been that night.

Pleasure built, a tidal wave that rocked them together, in unison, their breath and cries in perfect sync, so the moment her muscles began to spasm with uncontrollable pleasure, he exploded, burying himself in her with a guttural cry, kissing her hard, silencing her even as he devoured her voice, her impatience, her frantic need.

Like any natural disaster, there was the aftermath to contend with, and for Alejandro it was every bit as dangerous as the first time they'd slept together. He had crossed a line. Not once, but twice, and it was a line he'd thought he'd always, always respect: his friendship with Luca. He'd betrayed that friendship, and the knowledge sat like a stone in his gut because, even while being aware of it, he couldn't summon the remorse he deserved to feel.

He could no longer put an obligation to Luca above the wishes Sienna had clearly expressed. She was a grown woman, who had every right to explore her sexuality, to choose who she slept with and when. And she'd chosen him. He knew Luca's request came from a place of concern, but he also understood that Luca wasn't seeing Sienna as she really was. The picture he'd painted of a woman in need of protection was a far cry from the strong, independent woman who'd come to Alejandro's office and asked him to make love to her again. Admiration shifted through him as he contemplated what that must have taken.

'That was…'

She searched for a word, her eyes twinkling so he found himself smiling—and amusement was not a reaction he usually associated with sex but one he felt now, nonetheless.

'Yes.' Because there was no one single adjective that could do justice to what they'd shared. It was better to simply acknowledge they'd both been rocked by it.

It wasn't that Alejandro had grown bored of sex, so much as of his usual partners, who were so practised in seduction, so predictable. Or perhaps *he'd* grown predictable. He couldn't remember the last time he'd let passion move him to the point he took a woman on a desk. Or a sofa in a restaurant powder room, for that matter.

'How long are you in Barcelona for?'

'I'm booked to fly out later tonight, actually.' He braced his palms on the desk, on either side of her, keeping the irritation blocked from his face.

'So that is all you wanted from me?'

She laughed softly. 'Oh, don't be hurt.' She lifted a finger and absent-mindedly traced one of his scars— gained when he was only thirteen years old, with the craggy edge of a broken bottle. 'I can change my flight.'

'I was not hurt,' he felt compelled to clarify. 'Simply surprised.'

'I didn't know if you'd agree.' She shrugged those creamy, delightful shoulders and her breasts harumphed in unison. He lifted his hands, cupping them, just as he'd wanted to from almost the first moment he'd met her. Her eyes flecked with a whirlwind of need. 'And if you did agree, well, suffice it to say, the logistics all seemed a little up in the air.'

'And now?'

'I suppose they still are.'

'Why?'

'Well, I have to get back to work at some point. I actually didn't think this through too well.' She expelled a breath so her hair lifted, brushing her forehead gently. 'Impulsiveness is my biggest downfall.'

'From where I'm standing, it's a virtue.' She laughed softly and before he knew it, he was grinning like a fool. 'Stay for the rest of the week.' The words were out before he could stop them and panic tightened in his chest. But he quelled it quickly. After all, that was only a few days, and it didn't mean they'd be spending every minute together. 'I will still have to work, but your nights will be mine...'

She hesitated. Having already crossed to the dark side by betraying his best friend, he felt only a hint of compunction in going all the way—he squeezed her nipples, watching unashamedly as pleasure darkened her cheeks.

He sucked her lower lip between his teeth, wobbled it there then dropped his head to one of her breasts, taking a nipple in his mouth and rolling it with his tongue. 'This is not negotiable. If we're going to do this, we're going to do it right, and that will take the week.'

The rest of the week! She felt giddy. She felt...a thousand and one things, actually. Relief, euphoria, delight, joy, satisfaction and hunger, all rolled into one. 'It's good to know the first time wasn't a fluke, though.'

Mock outrage shifted his features. 'You seriously thought it might have been?'

'Sorry to offend your sexual prowess.' She grinned, so he moved his attention back to her mouth, kissing her there, taking her breath away with each flick of his tongue until she saw stars.

'Believe me, I relish the opportunity to continue proving you wrong.'

'Or right. I'm not sure I actually thought it was a fluke, so much as I hoped that the repeat performance, if there even *was* a repeat performance, would live up to the experience.'

He laughed, a low, soft sound. 'You really are quite unique.'

'Why can't you be more like your sister? More like other girls?'

She sobered a moment, sitting a little straighter, pressing a hand to his chest. The ridges of his scar edged beneath her fingertip. 'What happened here?'

He didn't answer and when she looked up at him, his face had changed. A small smile tilted his lips but it didn't reach his eyes; it was an imitation, almost chilling. 'A childhood misadventure.'

'That you don't want to talk about,' she surmised. 'I understand.' She leaned forward and pressed a kiss to the edges. She understood all about scars—but hers were the kind you couldn't see. Nonetheless, they were scraped right across her heart and soul, and always would be. She didn't particularly want to talk about those either.

'It's not that I don't want to talk about it. It's no big deal. I got in a fight.'

'A fight you lost?'

'A fight I won, though my opponent saw fit to arm himself with a broken beer bottle.' He ran his own finger across the scar, a distracted look on his face, then lifted his finger to his neck, pointing to another scar, about an inch below his ear.

'My God, it's lucky he didn't get a major vein or artery.'

He lifted his shoulders. 'He didn't. I survived.'

A shiver ran down her spine. 'How old were you?'

'Thirteen.'

Concern shifted through her. 'Who was he?' She could only think of her own father in that moment, and how often she'd been afraid as a child. Not that she'd ever seen him hit her mother, but the way he'd yelled and loomed over her—over them all—had filled the same space in her brain. She'd hatched a thousand and one plans of how she'd defend them if and when he turned violent. She'd lived with that fear until the day her father died.

'Just some drunk.'

Sienna couldn't help herself. She kissed the edge of his scar again, imagining being thirteen years old and attacked by a rambling, violent alcoholic. How was it possible? Where were his parents?

He took a step back, separating them, his face a mask of professional cool. 'My driver is downstairs. He'll let you into my place.' Then, the cool gave way to fire, at least in his eyes, as he leaned forward, almost against his will, and kissed her. 'I'll be as quick as I can be.'

Sienna hadn't thought far enough ahead to know how she'd handle things *if* he accepted her offer. She supposed she'd imagined getting a hotel room, but from the moment he'd suggested she go back to his place curiosity had overwhelmed her, and temptation too, so she'd simply nodded, even when alarm sirens had been sounding through her brain.

Her mother had always acquiesced to their father and Sienna had sworn she'd never be like that. But this wasn't a big deal. Alejandro wasn't a man she intended to date. He certainly wasn't the man she would end up marrying, and, furthermore, his suggestion made sense. She could stay at his place for tonight at least, and then come up with a firmer plan the next day.

His driver was a handsome man named Raul, who

looked as if he practised hardcore wrestling in his spare time. His arms were wider than her head's circumference. When he spoke, his voice was gentle, though, and he opened the door for her with a kindly smile, which made her wonder how often Raul was asked to escort women home. She pushed the question aside. She already had the answer to that. Alejandro was a prolific bachelor. That was part of why she'd hatched this plan. She *liked* that she was just another notch on the bedpost to him. She liked that she could share this experience with someone who would likely forget all about her, leaving her free to focus on finding a suitable groom and planning the wedding, when the time came.

Barcelona was stunning. She focussed on the city as the car cut through traffic, the buildings a charming mix of old and new, the prominent Gaudí architecture eye-catching whenever they rounded a corner and one of his masterpieces sprung almost organically from the pavement. The sun was high in the sky, the heat of the day unrelenting, so she was grateful for the car's powerful air-conditioner and tinted windows. Nonetheless, when they passed an ice-cream cart her mouth went dry from the force of her temptation. She stared at it as they passed, wishing she could trade places, just for a moment, with the children playing around it, their hands outstretched for the delicious treat.

The car drove on, turning into a wide boulevard with verdant trees lining either side, creating a canopy of shade for the generous footpaths. The buildings here were almost all old, stunningly ornate, many with either shops or cafes underneath them, so people spilled out, the sound of their laughter permeating the vehicle when they pulled up at traffic lights. The elegance of their dress made Sienna's heart tremble almost to a stop. She looked down at the summery dress she'd pulled on this morning—one of her favourites—and grimaced.

She was as far removed from Spanish chic as it was possible to get.

Unbidden, the images—hundreds of images—of Alejandro's former lovers flashed into her mind, adding to the pool of unease she always felt about her appearance. Oh, she was self-aware enough to know that her mother bore the blame for that completely. She also knew she wasn't as overweight and unattractive as her mother liked to taunt. But nor was she svelte and glamorous like Olivia and Angelica. She was pale-skinned with freckles and auburn hair, and even though her puppy fat had left her when she'd outgrown adolescence, her breasts and hips hadn't got the memo, remaining steadfastly curvaceous, meaning it was difficult to find dresses that fitted because the waists were invariably far too loose if she bought anything that actually suited her bust line.

Except for dresses like this—loose and floaty and somehow freeing.

But definitely not chic.

Definitely not Alejandro Corderó chic.

The car began to move again, sliding along the street. She caught a sign as they went—Passeig de Gràcia—and vaguely recalled having seen an article about this place in one of her mother's high-end fashion magazines. They passed boutiques now, designer names visible between the trunks of the trees, the clientele obviously sophisticated and monied.

Sienna sat back in her seat, trying to stave off the sense of panic. She felt as though she'd stepped into a completely foreign world, and she had no idea what she was doing here. Despite the temptation to stay, she had a stronger urge, albeit brief, to beg Raul to take her to the airport instead.

But Alejandro…

Her stomach flip-flopped so she gripped the handle in the car door, frowning a little as her eyes continued to run over the streetscape without taking in any of the details now.

It wasn't just Alejandro. It was Sienna too. She'd made this choice; she'd chosen to do this because she deserved it. She had never questioned her fate: marriage, as dictated by her father—only she'd long ago started to see her marriage as a form of revenge. He'd been seeking control, but she was going to take the money and use it in a way that he would *hate*. Her marriage was no longer a source of despair for Sienna, but a prospect she relished, because in making the match she could take back her power, could exercise control over her own life, in a way her dictatorial father would have never envisaged. But this was the ice cream on the cake. Another exercise of control, a way to walk her own path, to live her own life, away from the cloying confines of Hughenwood House.

Raul slowed the car, then turned into a side street, pulling to a stop in a driveway. A man in a suit appeared, a concierge.

'Good afternoon.' He opened the door for her.

'Hello.' She slipped into Spanish effortlessly.

'Would you show Senyor Corderó's guest to his apartment?'

'Of course.' The concierge gestured towards the doors—wide, glass, rimmed with thick gold frames.

'My bag.' She reached into the car but the concierge was faster, lifting it by the strap and holding it, so she couldn't help but notice how tatty her holdall was.

'Thank you.' She turned to Raul and smiled. 'I'll see you later.'

He nodded once. Was that scepticism in his eyes? Fair enough. She supposed the women he drove home didn't generally make repeat appearances.

Falling into step behind the concierge, she couldn't help the little gasp that escaped her lips when they entered the foyer. Polished white tiles covered the entire floor, then gave way to walls that were wallpapered in gold and white stripes, a ceiling that was ornately patterned, and enormous chandeliers that hung in a line across the room. The ceilings themselves were at least treble height, creating an elegant and enormous space.

All for a lobby!

There were vases too, copper, overflowing with flowers—as they passed she breathed in and their fragrance was almost intoxicating. Lilies, bluebells and jasmine were surrounded by glossy green foliage.

'Senyor Corderó's apartment is at the top. Did he provide you with a card?'

She stared at him blankly for a moment before she remembered that, yes, he had pressed something into her hand as she was leaving. She'd just been too flummoxed by the reality of what was happening to take it in.

'Oh, yes,' she agreed, nodding towards the bag. 'In there.'

The concierge passed the backpack over. She unzipped the front pocket and removed the piece of plastic.

'Swipe it here.' He indicated a slot, then stepped out of the lift. A second later, the doors pinged shut. She did as he'd said, then the lift was whooshing upwards. A mirror on the side wall caught her attention before she could realise it was there, and she saw the image she made and could only stare.

She looked...wild. Wanton. Her mother would definitely not approve. The thought brought a smile to her lips, a genuine one, because it was her secret, and yet the fact her mother wouldn't have approved—and wouldn't have believed it—was a definite silver lining. It was Sienna's life, her prerogative, and she loved knowing that she was doing something no one would have thought her capable of.

The doors pinged open, not into a corridor as she'd expected, but into a grandiose entrance foyer that gave way to a room positively bursting with light. The south-facing windows bathed the room in afternoon gold, the floor-to-ceiling glass showcasing a stunning outlook—of a large shrub-lined terrace and, beyond it, the varied roofs of the boulevard. Despite the fact her arrival was unexpected, the place was immaculate. In fact, it looked barely lived in. She grimaced at her rustic backpack once more, placing it by the door and trying not to register how out of place it was, before placing her sandals beside it and padding, barefoot, into the lounge room.

It expanded around her: huge, white, overwhelming, beautiful. Everything was the palest of wood or cream, except for a grand piano towards the left, which was dark and highly polished. She moved towards it and pressed a series of keys, wondering if Alejandro played or if it was purely decorative.

Somehow, she couldn't imagine him doing something so ordinary as playing the piano, and yet just imagining him sitting here, shirtless, bathed in the light of the moon, made her heart skip a beat.

There was nothing to do but explore, and so Sienna wandered from room to room, each decorated like a six-star hotel, with barely a hint of personal effects, so it took guesswork to establish which of the three bedrooms was actually Alejandro's—eventually she picked it because the bed was largest and there was, on closer inspection, a newspaper on the bedside table.

A small hint, but enough. She didn't linger in the room. It felt too invasive, despite what she'd come here for.

There were other rooms, which she supposed might have been bedrooms at one point, but which had been converted into other purposes, more suited to Alejandro. There was a state-of-the-art office, with screens mounted on the wall, a large, dark desk, and a leather armchair. It provided a view of the terrace, including the infinity pool in the corner. She stared at it with a deep yearning—how long had it been since she'd gone swimming? As girls, they'd always swum in the lake at Hughenwood House, but without the gardening staff, it had quickly become overgrown with lily pads and slimy algae, not safe to use any longer, and so the pursuit had been abandoned. The turquoise water of this pool looked irresistible.

She stepped out of his office, passing another room—
a gymnasium with a boxing ring in the centre—and
moved back into the lounge area, wishing she'd brought
bathers with her. But why would she have?

She cast a glance about the penthouse somewhat
guiltily and then, with another bright, defiant smile
tilting her lips, Sienna disappeared onto the terrace,
shedding clothes as she got closer and closer to the infinity pool.

CHAPTER SEVEN

He'd concluded the meeting as swiftly as he could, but that had still meant he was delayed by almost an hour, and it was only as Raul pulled up in front of his apartment building that Alejandro wondered what Sienna had been doing to keep busy. She had her phone, so perhaps she'd spent the time scrolling Instagram or similar, but something about that didn't fit right. For some reason, he couldn't see her as someone who spent a lot of time on social media. Reading a book? Writing emails? He frowned, wondering at how little he knew of her, and why that felt strange. He didn't exactly go around collecting the biographies of the women he slept with, so why should she be any different? Because the few things he *did* know about her had sparked a billion fresh questions, and Alejandro liked having answers to his questions.

He'd grappled with his guilt on the drive to the apartment. It still sat inside him, and he doubted it would ever shift—on some level, he was glad for that. To not feel bad for having betrayed his oldest friend would have spoken volumes about his character. He didn't want to hurt Luca. But this was no longer about his friend.

Sienna was her own person, with her own autonomy. Alejandro couldn't refuse her simply because Luca had misread her character and needs.

He pushed into his apartment, looking around, frowning. For a moment, he thought she wasn't here, but her rucksack was by the door, as well as her strappy shoes. His eyes scanned the lounge area, and he moved through it, unbuttoning his shirt at the neck, rolling up the sleeves as he scanned the room for a clue of her whereabouts.

Curiosity growing, he continued to move through the apartment, room by room, until he passed his office and a movement, a splash, caught his eye.

He stopped walking.

And stared.

She was in the pool.

And going by the trail of clothes between him and the pool, she was naked.

Despite the fact they'd made love earlier that afternoon, desire burst through him like volcanic lava. He cut through his office, opening the French doors onto the terrace and startling her, apparently, with his abrupt arrival. Almost as though she hadn't expected him, as though she hadn't been swimming naked with the specific intent of tempting him...

'Alejandro.' She breathed his name, her body instantly heating in response despite the water lapping at her sides. Instinctively, she ducked down, so only her head and neck sat above the water's surface. It was no good, though. His eyes clung to her creamy breasts beneath

the rippling water, feasting on their outline, so she expelled a soft breath, her eyes clinging to his.

'Well, this is a nice surprise,' he drawled.

She looked around desperately for her clothes—flung
with careless non-concern across the tiles of the deck.

'I wasn't sure what time you'd be here,' she murmured. 'I thought much later, to be honest.'

'I'm disappointed. Are you telling me this display
isn't to tempt me?'

Her eyes widened. Tempt him? 'Sorry to disappoint,
but that didn't even occur to me.'

His laugh was soft and ran like melted butter across
her skin. She shivered despite the heat of the afternoon.

'If you'll pass me a towel, I'll get out.'

'Get out?' He shook his head. 'I don't think so.' And
with her eyes feasting on his body, he undressed, slowly,
purposefully, as if he knew what torment the gradual reveal of his naked frame was doing to her equilibrium. In
reality, it took him less than a minute to strip out of his
shirt and trousers, but to her disappointment he left his
boxers on, diving into the pool with a power that took
her breath away. Seconds later, he was right where she
was, lifting up just an inch away, his dark hair slicked
back from his brow, his eyes glowing with a thousand
shades of blue in the afternoon light.

'Much more fun to stay in together, no?'

There was so much she didn't know about him, but
one thing she did was that his accent grew thicker when
he was flirting. The words softened and ran over her
like velvet, so her nipples tingled, silently begging for
his touch.

'Definitely.'

Another laugh. 'I'm glad you agree.'

'This place is something else.'

He looked around the expansive terrace, as if seeing it from her eyes. 'I suppose so.'

'You're just used to it.' She pulled away from him, not because she wanted to, but because her body was heating with a need she couldn't control, and she knew, from recent experience, that physical distance was the only way to contain that. 'But, trust me, it's incredible.'

He was quiet, but she knew he was coming, following her, so that when she braced her elbows on the edge of the pool, looking down at the street below, he was right beside her in an instant. So much for distance. So much for *wanting* distance. Her traitorous body felt as though it were partly on fire, and she ached to reach out and touch him.

'When did you move here?' Talking was good. Talking distracted her. Sort of.

'I bought the place about six years ago, and I spend my time between here and Madrid.'

'You have a place there too?'

He nodded.

'As nice as this?'

A smile made his lips tilt off kilter. 'Different.'

'Ah. A man of mystery.'

'Always.'

'Tell me this, then.' She turned to face him, and he capitalised on her shift, pulling her closer, tucking his hands around her bottom and keeping them there. Her eyes dropped closed for an instant, because the sensation and intimacy of it was almost too much.

'*Sí?*'

'Do you actually play the piano, or is it a prop to impress guests?'

He grinned. 'Do you think I'm the kind of man who gives a crap what anyone thinks of me?'

She tilted her head to the side, considering that. 'No.'

'So you already have your answer.'

'When did you learn?'

She was making conversation simply because she was nervous, but at the same time she found she was truly interested in understanding him. It should have been a warning, but Sienna was beyond the point of heeding those. 'At school.'

Another thing she knew about Alejandro—he brushed aside questions he didn't want to answer. He acted as though they didn't matter, yet that was a tip that they really did.

'Do you enjoy it?'

He considered that. 'I suppose so. I never thought about it in those terms. It's simply something I do.'

'I'd like to hear you play.'

'Why?'

'Because I imagined you playing when I walked into your sky palace and saw the piano, and, I have to admit, my imagination found the image kind of sexy.'

He laughed. 'I see.'

'What do you play?' She lifted a hand to his hair when she found she could no longer stop herself from touching him. Her fingers ran through its length, her eyes following the gesture, then her hand fell to his shoulder, warm and smooth, strong and fascinating.

'Classical music.'

'Not rock?'

He shook his head. 'Not often.'

'That's strange. You definitely strike me as more Metallica than Mozart.'

'Perhaps in some ways.'

'A penchant for black leather pants?'

'On some people.'

She looked away, cheeks flaming. He wasn't talking about *her*. Leather pants would make her bottom look the size of Alaska, and then some.

He caught her chin, drawing her face back towards him. 'You don't approve?'

'It's not really my thing.' Oh, dear. Her voice sounded so prim—and she definitely wasn't that. She forced a smile to lessen the impact. 'But I dare say most of the women you, um, bring back here…'

A small line formed between his brows when he frowned, and she stared at it, fascinated. But she didn't want to talk about his ex-lovers, nor to really even think about them. They were irrelevant.

'Actually, I don't bring women to my home.'

She blinked at him, surprised and, she hated to admit it, a little flattered. 'Why not?'

'Because they either have homes of their own, or hotel rooms, or because I'm travelling myself.' He lifted his shoulders. 'These circumstances are quite rare.'

'I can rent a hotel room,' she said immediately, pride firing to life. 'That was always my plan, if you were to agree—'

'It makes no sense.' He waved aside the offer. 'My place is big enough to share.'

Her heart skipped a beat. Share. Why did that word sound so…romantic? She pushed the word aside.

Romance had nothing to do with it. This was a week of sexploration and nothing more. To prove her point, she closed the distance between them completely, pressing her naked breasts to his chest, moving her hips slightly beneath the water. His only response was a slight dilation of his pupils, and a hardening of his cock against her belly. She dug her nails into his shoulder a little, need flashing white-hot through her.

'And I won't stay long,' she said quietly, still not ruling out the idea of leaving for a hotel the next day.

He lifted his shoulders. 'I work long hours.' His hands moved from her bottom, one straying to her hip, the other finding the sensitive flesh of her sex and exploring it slowly, before sliding a finger inside her moist core. She moaned softly. 'It is only the nights when we will see one another—and these, I believe we have agreed, we will enjoy spending together.'

'Yes,' she whimpered, not sure what she was responding to, only that the word felt perfectly, perfectly right. He withdrew his finger, his eyes watching her, looking at her, and the power of his gaze was its own aphrodisiac, so pleasure built inside her, warm and irresistible, euphoria-inducing.

'You are beautiful when you're close to coming.'

She shook her head instinctively. She didn't need the flattery. Beauty wasn't something she'd ever aspired to, and it wasn't an adjective she needed to hear employed. 'Just don't stop,' she ground out, moving her hips down, inviting him, needing him.

He made a throaty sound—a laugh?—and moved faster, so she tilted her head back, riding a wave, as he kissed the sensitive flesh at the base of her neck, sucking her there, marking her, so a thrill of pleasure ran the length of her spine along with the deluge of release that was racking her body. 'I feel as though I've died and gone to heaven,' she said honestly, when she could breathe again, and string at least a few words together.

'Don't die,' he responded with a grin. Her hand moved beneath the water, and the sensation was heightened by nerve endings that were over-stimulated. She brushed her fingertips over his arousal, rock-hard against the wet fabric of his underpants. She was shy, of course, because she had no experience with this, but at the same time she was emboldened by what they'd shared, and by the proof she'd just felt that he was as into her as she was to him. 'I want you.'

His eyes widened. 'I know.'

She should have been embarrassed; she wasn't.

'And? Are you going to do anything about it?'

'Soon.' He leaned forward, kissing her slowly, and she relaxed into the kiss, their bodies melded, his hardness against her belly a reminder that this was just the beginning.

'Now?'

Another laugh. 'Not without protection.'

She pulled back, staring at him, startled that she'd forgotten something so basic. 'I didn't even think—'

His shrug was nonchalant. 'You're not used to having to consider such things.'

'No, but still…'

'It's fine.'

She bit down on her lip. 'I'm on the pill.'

'You told me that. Since when?'

'Um, about a day after we—'

He lifted a brow. 'Because you thought this might happen?'

'Because I thought I should be more prepared.'

'Ah.' His smile sent butterflies rampaging through her stomach.

'I just meant, if you wanted, we could—'

He scanned her face, his eyes moving slowly, and then he shook his head. 'There is still a risk of conceiving, and I am not prepared to take any chances. Double protection is better.'

'You really must not want kids,' she said with a hint of humour, to cover her disappointment. Not about children, of course, but because her desire was so strong she found she didn't much fancy waiting—even a short while.

'I don't want to make a woman pregnant.'

She frowned. 'Isn't that the same thing?'

'No.'

'So you do want children, just not unplanned ones?'

'I wouldn't say that, either.'

She laughed huskily. 'You're not making any sense, but that's okay. I don't really need you to explain it to me.'

He nodded, but there was thoughtfulness in his gaze, and a moment later he continued. 'I don't want children, under any circumstances, because I believe a child should be raised by two parents, wherever possible. And I'm not interested in that kind of relationship. Up until a few months ago, I would have said that outlook was one of the many things Luca and I have in common.'

'Oh?'

But he compressed his lips, turning to face the view

rather than expand on that thought. Only Sienna was just as protective of Olivia as Olivia was of Sienna, and she wasn't ready to let the matter drop. 'I know he's dated a heap of women. Actresses, models and the like.'

Alejandro made a grunting noise of agreement.

'So I guess leopards can change their spots after all.'

'Some can, evidently.' He turned to face her, pinning her with eyes that seemed to bore right through her soul. 'But not me.'

Something cool stole through her, replacing the warmth he'd so easily flared in her body. 'Do you think he's really changed?'

Alejandro's eyes narrowed. 'You're worried about your sister?'

'Wouldn't you be?'

'Not for one second.'

'But you just said...'

'Luca isn't the kind of man who would do anything half-heartedly. They're married. It's quite clear he loves her.'

Sienna turned, her eyes landing on the street below, uncertainty a spiral in her belly. 'They do *seem* happy.'

'But you are not convinced.'

She kept her gaze averted, wondering at the way she felt as though she could speak so freely to Alejandro, given that they barely knew one another. Was it his friendship with Luca? Or the fact that they'd agreed this would be over in a few nights?

'Did Luca tell you about the will?'

'What will?'

That, then, was her answer. 'Our father's.'

'I only know your father is not alive because he

wasn't at the wedding, and when I mentioned it to Luca he said, very matter-of-factly, that he's dead. In fact, he said "The bastard is dead", so I presume there is bad blood between your sister and father.'

Sienna's smile was like ice. 'You could say that.'

'And this somehow impacts their marriage?'

Her eyes lifted to his and she tried to work out if it was madness to confide in him, but something drew her closer, making it impossible to shut the conversation down. 'Perhaps it's better if I explain how my father's will affects me,' she said thoughtfully. It was the middle ground, allowing her to speak openly, without betraying her sister. 'You can draw your own conclusions as to Luca and Olivia and my...concerns.'

But where to begin? Her father's arcane beliefs were almost impossible to express. They were so divorced from any kind of reality, Sienna felt a familiar flush of shame that she experienced whenever she was forced to admit the implications of the legal arrangements.

'My parents' marriage wasn't what you'd describe as happy. They met when my mother was really young, Dad was almost twenty years older. She was an actress and used to being adored. She was, of course, very beautiful.' Sienna kept any hint of bitterness from her voice—she'd long ago grown accustomed to the genetics lottery and how it had skipped her. 'My father doted on her, I gather, in the early days. But she was young, and she made a mistake.'

'A mistake?'

'An affair,' Sienna filled in the gap. 'It was with some director she'd known before she met Dad. She regretted it.'

'They seem to have told you a lot about their private lives.'

'Screamed it at the top of their lungs, more like, during fights.' She angled a face at him, a soft, sad smile catching on her lips. 'He never forgave her. But not only did he not forgive her, he didn't let her go. He hated her, but he also loved her, in a sick, unhealthy kind of way, so he would criticise her and demean her, controlled all the family's finances so she had no ability to travel or do anything without asking him for money.'

'Why did she stay?'

'Because she "loved" him.' Sienna lifted her fingers to do air quotations, showing her cynicism for the idea of love.

'You think love is a lie?'

'I think it's a flawed concept,' she corrected. 'How can you love someone if you don't also respect them enough to treat them well? How can you love someone if you don't want to make them happy?'

'And she was unhappy?'

'We all were.' Her lips tightened into a grimace. 'They fought often, and when they weren't fighting, he was giving her the silent treatment, so we were all trying our best to walk on eggshells, hoping to avoid sparking the next outburst. And walking on eggshells is not something I'm very good at.' Her brows furrowed. 'I used to try to ease the tension, to get everyone talking, or, better yet, laughing, but it never helped. Olivia was much better at reading the room than me. She knew when to keep her head down, when to make herself scarce.'

'And you didn't?'

'I *did* run away a lot.'

'Seriously?'

'Well, no.' Now a genuine smile softened her features. 'I ran, but only to Gertie's house.'

'Gertie?'

'The woman who's looking after my dog. You met her at the wedding. She's Andrew's grandmother, and she lives just over a field from Hughenwood House—our family property. I used to go to her house when things got bad, and she'd make me scones and biscuits and cake and tea with three lumps of sugar, all of the treats Mum had banned from the house in an effort to stay looking perennially young.' She rolled her eyes. 'Gertie would let me hide out for a while, talk it out, then send me home with a piece of cake wrapped in a napkin. She was my saviour as a kid.'

'And you're still close?'

'Very.' Sienna tilted her head back, wetting her hair, then pulled it over her shoulder. For a moment, she'd forgotten she was stark naked, but the moment her hair collided with her breast she startled, fighting a ridiculous urge to cover herself. 'I wanted to go to uni, but it wasn't possible. Gertie introduced Andrew and me and he created a spot in his charities team. It's been an amazing experience.'

'I can imagine.' Was that cynicism in his voice? Of course not. She ignored the doubt, running a finger over the pool's coping.

'Anyway. My father passed away when I was eleven. It was completely unexpected—a heart attack. And Mum, rather than being able to start living her life again, was restricted because of his bloody will. I actually don't even know how the bloody thing is legal, but Andrew's looked into it for me, and apparently it's airtight.'

His features gave nothing away. 'Tell me about it.'

She sucked in a deep breath. 'Well, basically, Mum didn't inherit anything from Dad. He was such a bastard to her, right to the very end. His estate pays a small stipend, and she's entitled to live in Hughenwood House until we turn twenty-five or get married. Once we get married, so long as we do so before we turn twenty-five, the house passes to us, as well as a financial settlement.'

His features tightened into a mask of steel. 'Let me repeat that, to be sure I've understood. You are saying that your father died when you were just a girl, but somehow he saw fit to make sure you would be denied any inheritance unless you were married?'

She nodded once.

'What if you have no interest in marrying?'

'Which, given what I grew up experiencing, I don't, particularly.'

'Right. And so?'

'But in order to inherit, I must.'

He compressed his lips. 'Then screw it. Walk away from the money.'

'I can't do that.'

'Why not? You'd rather take the money even when it means allowing your father to dictate this to you from beyond the grave?'

'I'd rather take the money than let him win.'

'Isn't marrying for the sake of the will handing him that victory?'

Her eyes sparked with his. 'No.'

'Why not?'

'Because of what I intend to do with the money.'

'Which is? Burn him in effigy a thousand times over?'

'Something much more satisfying,' she promised. 'I'm going to donate the money—all of it—to a charity that works with domestic violence survivors, enabling them to start over.'

He considered that for several beats. 'As revenge on your father?'

'When I'm feeling mature, I think of it as simply doing the right thing.'

Alejandro's eyes scanned hers, probing her, reading her, and she thought, for a moment, that he was going to say something, but he held himself back, lifting a finger to her cheek instead, the contact sending a thousand shock waves through her body. 'And you believe this is why my friend married your sister?'

'Oh, I know it's why they married. The question is, is it why they're *still* married?'

'I do not believe so.'

'No?'

'Luca told me he loves her. He told me he would die for her. In fact, he told me that it is only since meeting your sister he has realised that he was never really living at all. I believe him fully capable of marrying a woman to help her escape poverty and oppression, but not to gilding the lily to that extent. He loves her, *querida*. He would not lie to me about this, or anything.' And for a moment, the light went out in Alejandro's blue eyes, so they looked almost grey, and tension flooded his body.

Sienna didn't take too much notice. She expelled a

soft breath, relief wrapping around her. 'I hope you're right.'

'I am.' And after a small pause, a brief hesitation, he kissed her, gently, the warmth from the sun and the water and his lips pushing all unpleasant thoughts from her mind, leaving only, for a little while, happiness.

CHAPTER EIGHT

'CORDERÓ.' HE ANSWERED the call without checking who was ringing, not wanting to risk the buzzing of his phone waking Sienna, who'd only fallen asleep a while earlier. He cast her a glance as he slipped from the room, her red hair spread like flames across his crisp white pillows, her body naked, half concealed by the sheet, one leg sticking out tempting him to go back to bed, to begin kissing her on her toes and working his way up...

But it was late, and she must be exhausted, given how they'd spent the last few hours.

He pulled the door closed softly behind him, moving into the corridor and towards the kitchen, as the voice on the other end of the line spoke.

'Alex, how are you?'

He stopped walking, closing his eyes on a wave of guilt.

'Luca. Fine. You?'

'Yeah, all good. I haven't had a chance to check in with you since the wedding. We've been busy.'

'You're on your honeymoon, I hope I'm the last thing on your mind.'

'Right.' Luca's laugh was natural and relaxed, so even if Sienna's revelations the afternoon before had given Alejandro a moment's worry, the sound of his friend's voice alleviated it completely.

'I wanted you to be one of the first to know: Olivia's pregnant.'

Alejandro reached for the coffee grinds and scooped some into his pot, adding water then placing it on top of the stove, the words dropping through him like stones. Marriage. And now children? 'Who are you and what have you done with Luca?'

'What do you mean?'

'You sound happy.'

'I am.'

Alejandro braced his palms on the counter, his gaze lazily tracing another scar, which ran from his thumb across the back of his hand down to his wrist. That one had been from a flick knife. 'Then so am I.'

'I'll take that as congratulations.'

'As it was intended.'

'I also wanted to thank you.'

'What for?' Alejandro reached for a small cup, moving towards the stove and watching as flames licked the sides of the coffeepot.

'For taking care of Sienna at the wedding. Olivia's very protective of her, which means I am too, and their mother is such a bitch. She's a beautiful girl. I hated seeing her so tense at the wedding.'

Alejandro closed his eyes on another roll of guilt. Tell him the truth. Tell him it was your pleasure. That, actually, it went beyond just looking after her. Tell him Sienna isn't his responsibility, that she can make her own decisions in life, that what they were doing was none of Luca's business.

'Sure.'

'Don't sound so happy about it.'

Alejandro frowned, not liking the implication of that, but not knowing how to defend himself—and Sienna—without being frank about exactly how happy he'd been. 'It was no problem,' he tried again. 'I enjoyed meeting her.'

'Good. You'll probably see a bit more of her, given that you're both going to be godparents to our first child.'

'What?'

'You can skip being my best man, but not my child's godfather. Sorry, it is not negotiable.'

Guilt was now a full-blown explosion at the base of his chest. He'd known Sienna would be someone he'd see, from time to time, in some capacity, given her connection to Luca, but sharing godparent duties?

He flicked off the flames abruptly, reaching for the pot and filling his cup with the dark, fragranced liquid. 'I'm not religious.'

'You are a good man. The best man I know. There is no one I would rather have guiding my child in times of darkness. You know that.'

Guilt clawed through him. 'Have you told Sienna yet?'

'No. Why? Do you want to do it?' Luca laughed, apparently oblivious to the slip Alejandro had just made—a question that had made it seem he, Alejandro, was in ongoing contact with Sienna.

'I was just curious.' Lying was not something Alejandro did well. It was not something he had done in a very long time, since he'd been forced into stealing food to survive. He hated this, and he particularly hated lying to Luca. But the situation was too messy to see a way out of. Besides, Sienna had sworn him to secrecy. Even if he wanted to tell Luca what was going on, he couldn't without betraying her trust. And so what was his option? To betray Luca's trust instead?

'Olivia's going to wait until they catch up next month. She wants to do it in person.'

'Got it.'

'So if you should happen to run into her, mum's the word.'

'Why is Olivia so protective of Sienna?'

The question was out before he could stop it. He winced, wishing he hadn't asked it, but at the same time he stood very still, awaiting the response.

'Typical older sister stuff.' There was a note of restraint in Luca's voice and Alejandro understood. There was more his friend wasn't saying, secrets he considered private, shared between a wife and her husband. In some ways, it alleviated Alejandro's guilt a little, because if Luca could have secrets, so could Alejandro. Except Luca was simply protecting his wife's privacy, whereas Alejandro was indulging his ravenous libido because opportunity had come knocking. Because no woman since Sienna had been able to inspire his interest, and he'd been at risk of turning into stone until she came into his office with her very attractive proposition.

So what? That justified this?

But when he remembered the way she'd looked at him, the hope shimmering in her eyes, the uncertainty and raw, unshaped desire, he knew he'd make the same decision every single time. It might be wrong, it might be a betrayal of Luca, but it was, in so many other ways, completely right.

'Anyway, I just wanted to let you know. Our family's growing.'

Our family. That was what they were—like brothers. 'Congratulations, Luc. I'm truly thrilled for you.'

He disconnected the call and dropped the phone onto the benchtop as though it were a venomous snake primed to bite him. He carried his coffee onto the terrace, gravitating towards the swimming pool, remembering how she'd looked in the water, and as he'd lifted her out of it, her creamy skin glossed by moisture, little droplets running over her that he chased with his tongue as he carried her to one of the sun loungers, placing her down on it and kissing her until she was a pool of desire beneath him. Her responsiveness was the hottest thing he'd ever known. She melted when he touched her, and he sparked into flame and fire.

So how did he stop what they were doing from destroying his relationship from Luca?

It didn't matter that Luca would never know. Alejandro had to draw up his own boundaries, to make sure he was able to defend his actions, if the time ever came. So how did he do that?

By making sure he was looking after Sienna. Treating her well. And being completely honest with her, which he had been, right from the start. This was no prelude to love. There was no relationship in the offing, for either of them. Neither wanted that. But he had to make sure she didn't forget. He had to make sure the lines stayed in place, and that they both respected them. And when the week was over, he would move on, once and for all. No more fantasising about her. No more wanting her. And definitely no contacting her. Hers was one number that wouldn't be making it into Alejandro's little black book.

Light streamed into the palatial bedroom, waking Sienna some time before seven. She stretched in bed, languid and relaxed, her hands reaching out on autopilot for Alejandro, wanting him in a way that made her blush, particularly given how they'd spent most of the night before. How was it possible she craved him again already? Her hand ran over her nipples and she breathed out heavily, desire snaking through her. Where was he? She sat up, holding the sheet above her breasts, scanning the room. It was clear he wasn't there; the attached bathroom was silent. Frowning, she pushed her feet out of bed, standing, wrapping the sheet around her as an afterthought as she moved through the bedroom and into the corridor, ears straining for some sight or sound of him.

He was in the kitchen, eating a piece of toast. She paused, watching him for a moment before he became aware of her and looked up, his eyes roaming her with undisguised hunger.

'Good morning.'

'Bon dia.'

'You speak Catalan instead of Spanish?'

'I speak both.' His eyes narrowed. 'You're familiar with the languages?'

'Spanish,' she murmured, her stomach flipping and

flopping as she drew closer. She'd studied languages voraciously as a teen—Spanish, French, Italian and German, anything to blot out the silence and tension of her home life. 'Not Catalan. Want to teach me?'

'In a few days? Perhaps a few phrases.'

She ignored the odd lurching feeling at his reference to a few days. It was what they'd agreed. 'I'm an excellent student.'

'And yet, there are other things I'd prefer to help you learn.'

Heat flushed through her. 'Ah.'

'You are also an excellent student of those.' He reached out, dislodging the sheet, his eyes lightly mocking as the fabric rustled to the floor. 'Better.' His approval sent a tingle of warmth through her body.

'I didn't know where you were. Or if there'd be staff around.'

'No staff. I like my privacy.'

She expelled a sigh. 'So who keeps the place this clean?'

'I live by myself, and work long enough hours to mean I'm rarely here. It's not hard.'

There were so many questions she wanted to ask him. Out of nowhere, Sienna wondered what it would have been like if they'd met differently. If he weren't Luca's friend, and if she hadn't resolved, a long time ago, that her husband would be someone gentle and soft, someone completely non-threatening—the exact opposite to her father. But even if that were the case, she wasn't the kind of woman he usually went out with. He'd have bored of her way, way too soon, and she'd likely have been left broken-hearted, if she were ever stupid enough to give him her heart. This was definitely for the best.

'You're wearing a suit.'

He glanced down at his arms then returned his blue-grey eyes to her face. 'You're observant.'

She rolled her eyes. 'Don't tease.'

'But it's so fun.' He snaked out a hand and caught her at the waist, pulling her towards him. 'Will you still be naked tonight?'

'Waiting for you in the pool, you mean?'

'Excellent.' He nodded.

She laughed softly. 'That was not intended as a confirmation.'

He tilted her face up. 'That won't stop me imagining. Dreaming.'

'Hoping?'

'I never hope on other people's actions.'

'Too much room for disappointment?'

'Something like that.'

'You're a cynic.'

'Yes.'

Her breath was growing thick, hard to control, and her lungs hurt from the effort, as though she'd run a marathon.

'Raul's number is on the fridge.' His hand rose to her breast, stroking it possessively. 'Call him if you'd like to go anywhere in particular.'

She blinked, the desire he was invoking so easily at war with the words he was speaking. 'You're leaving?' It was the only conclusion.

'Yes.'

'So early?'

'This isn't early for me. It's when I always leave.'

And he wasn't about to change his plans for her. Message received. 'Got it.' She smiled, even when a strange lurching feeling gripped her stomach.

But he didn't leave. He stood there, touching her, looking at her, and she knew he was as tempted as she was. At least, she guessed he was, but after a moment he broke away, turning back to the kitchen and retrieving his jacket. He shrugged into it with all the panache of a male model.

'Text if you need anything.'

'I won't.'

He frowned. 'Good.' He hesitated again. Why? She wished she understood him better. 'I'll see you tonight.'

Not 'this afternoon'. Not even 'later'. Tonight. As in, after dark. For sex.

Just as they'd agreed.

She smiled brightly. 'Sounds good to me. See you later!'

There were approximately four million things Sienna would prefer to do than shop, particularly in a high-end place like the Passeig de Gràcia, but the simple fact was she was in need of clothes. She'd brought only enough for one night's stay, and though she could—and would—avail herself of the laundry facilities in Alejandro's apartment, there was also a feminine instinct flaring to life inside her, a desire to look her best, to absolutely wow him.

She strolled the street in the early afternoon sun, succumbing to an ice-cream vendor halfway down, choosing a small cone and eating it as she walked, the warmth of the day wrapping around her as the ice cream sought to bring cool and refreshment. She smiled, for no reason except that, in that moment, she felt abuzz with contentment. How could she not? Alejandro had set parts of her soul on fire that she hadn't even known existed, so for a moment she was able to push aside the worries that usually dogged her—worries that now included Olivia and her marriage. While their financial situation was considerably improved—Olivia had ploughed money into a bank account for Sienna and given her a credit card linked to it, telling her it was hers to do with what she wanted—Sienna still couldn't help but wonder if Olivia's marriage had come at too high a price.

Only Alejandro's voice was there, soothing those worries away, reminding her of what Luca had said, of his claim to love Olivia. And Sienna smiled, because it was impossible not to believe Alejandro, and if he was right, then it meant Olivia had got everything she wanted and deserved in life.

And Sienna?

Her marriage wouldn't be about love. She didn't want to run the risk of that. Oh, she was happy for Olivia, but falling in love—real, genuine, everlasting love—was like betting on a lightning strike landing at your feet. She wasn't going to risk her future happiness to something so unpredictable.

And sex?

Her heart skipped a beat, because a month ago the idea of a sexless, loveless marriage had seemed reassuringly practical. But now that Alejandro was bringing her to life, waking her up, she wondered if she could go back. Would she be satisfied without making love to her husband?

And what if her husband didn't invoke these same feelings in her? What if this was exceptionally good sex? She had no point of reference, but it was very easy to believe that Alejandro was a master at all that he did.

The thought stirred colour in her cheeks and she ducked between the doors of a department store with her head lowered, losing herself in the racks of nondescript clothes for the afternoon and trying not to think about Alejandro's mastery over her body—and how any other man might pale in comparison, even her husband…

'I thought we agreed you'd be naked.' His voice caught her completely off guard, but not her body. It flooded with hormones as though it had been waiting for him and was finally at ease.

She spun slowly, turning away from the glass windows that framed a view of the dusk-hued sky, her pulse throbbing when she saw him, so handsome in his suit, the way he looked at her sending a thousand sparks through her body.

'I've been out all afternoon. It didn't feel appropriate.'

He smiled appreciatively. 'Perhaps not. Though Barcelona is a very free society. Expression of self is encouraged.' His gaze raked her figure. 'However, I do like being the only man who's seen you naked.'

Heat at the possessive intent of his words spun through her like mini tornados.

'Even if that does puzzle me.' He was walking towards her, eyes hooked to hers, the look of intent only intensifying as he drew closer.

Her breath snagged in her throat, but she didn't take the easy path and look away; she couldn't. She was mesmerised by him.

'What does?'

'You're a very sexy, beautiful woman.' His fingers threaded beneath the straps of her dress, sending goosebumps running across her flesh. 'Surely there must have been times when you wanted to understand your body better.'

Her cheeks glowed. His fingers slid the dress down further. She shivered at the touch, so light, but somehow with the strength of a thousand thunderclaps.

'When I was a teenager, I had a few boyfriends, if you could call them that. Mum watched Olivia like a hawk—she was the beautiful one, the one Mum worried would be getting all the attention. Apparently, she didn't think there was much risk of that with me.'

His fingers crept to her back, unlatching her bra, so she forgot what she was saying. Even the feeling of it dropping away from her skin sent shock waves through her. Her nipples, so sensitive from last night's attention, tingled without having been so much as touched.

'So you were able to sneak around a little?' he prompted.

'A very little.' She bit down on her lip, memories of that time in her life unpleasant and troubling. 'It's really not worth discussing.'

But Alejandro wasn't someone to be easily put off the scent. 'Humour me.'

'What do you want to know?' She sighed dramati-

cally. 'My first kiss? A truly disastrous experience that
was more like eating eel than anything romantic. So
much tongue and wetness.' She shuddered for effect.
'My second kiss was not much better. I felt as though
he was trying to eat my face off.'

Alejandro's amusement was in the depths of his eyes,
but there was also a tightness there. 'And your third and
fourth kisses? Tell me you did not stop at two, *querida*?'

'Third was marginally better.' Hence, she'd allowed things to progress to the point he'd observed her
cantaloupe-sized breasts and all the criticism her mother
had poured into her teenage brain had flared to life, too
big to ignore.

'And?'

'And what?'

'It was a better kiss, but it stopped there?'

She hadn't expected such a direct question. She
opened her mouth then closed it, shaking her head.
'Does it matter?'

'You're humouring me, remember?'

'No, you're interrogating me.'

'Yes. But I promise I'll make it worth your while,
later.'

Later. 'No, now,' she demanded, surprising him, so
he laughed, a low, husky sound, before dropping his
lips, kissing her with the kind of mastery she could
never have known existed until a month ago. She trembled against him, wanting him with all of herself, needing him in a way that she was smart enough to know
was terrifying, because this was temporary and the need
couldn't be allowed to take hold of her.

He pulled away, leaving her head spinning, and her

heart thumping, his hands curving around her buttocks, holding her close to him, so she could feel the strength of his arousal. 'I have wanted you all day. I have been hard for you, waiting for this moment. But all day, there has been a question too, getting louder and louder, and I would like to know the answer.'

'But why?'

'So I can understand you.'

'Do you need to understand me? That sounds like boyfriend talk and that's definitely not what this is.'

A frown flickered across his handsome face. 'No, it's not.' Her heart twisted at his quick admission. 'But it's who I am. I need to know things, to get how they work.'

'I'm a thing now?' She joked to cover the strange blade of hurt pressing against her side.

'You're a person, but your issues are a thing.'

'How do you know this is an "issue"?'

'Because you're incredibly sensual. I cannot comprehend how you've denied this part of yourself for so long.'

Her stomach was in knots, desire at war with shame—yes, she felt shame, despite the fact she was now a grown woman who understood that her mother had bullied her all her life. Academic understanding of a situation didn't erase its impact—if only that were so!

'Of course, you don't understand. Look at you, Alejandro! Then look at me. There's no big mystery here.'

To his credit, he appeared to be genuinely lost. 'I don't understand.'

'You probably never went through an awkward teenage phase. I did. When Olivia hit adolescence, she went up. I went out. I put on weight, and got these huge breasts, and my mum—' But how to describe Angelica's particular brand of parenting? 'Let's just say, she didn't foster a healthy body image in anyone.'

Alejandro was still looking as though it didn't make any sense to him. 'But you were a teenager.'

'So?'

'So…' He shrugged in a way she found beyond sexy. 'Hormones, development, bodies change.'

'It's not just about my body. It's everything. My hair, my freckles, I'm the antithesis of my mother. Olivia was cast in her image and I'm some kind of throwback to my father's Irish grandmother.'

'Your hair is like flame.'

'It's okay. I've made my peace with my appearance.'

'What is there to make peace with?'

She stared at him, bemused. It was almost as though he genuinely didn't see how unglamorous she was. 'I looked you up online. I've seen the kind of women you usually date. I'm nothing like them. Please, don't treat me like an idiot and act as though you haven't noticed.'

'And do you think I'm not attracted to you?' He pushed his body forward, reminding her of the physical evidence of his desire.

'I don't know what I'm saying,' she said honestly, after a beat. 'But you asked and it's not an easy question to answer without unravelling all sorts of things I prefer not to think about.'

'Your mother criticised your appearance so often and so easily that you began to believe it. You still believe it. It robbed you of confidence, so you didn't want to share yourself with a partner.'

Her lips parted at the accuracy of his assessment,

and she heard herself admit something she'd wanted to keep private. 'There was one time.' She swallowed past a lump of bitter hurt. 'The third kiss. I liked him. But he—'

Alejandro tensed—as though bracing for her to confess something terrible, so she shook her head, quickly reassuring him.

'It wasn't serious. It's just, he—' She forced herself to be honest, and even to smile, because the passage of time helped her see the inept words in a different light. 'He compared my breasts to melons and I never quite got over that imagery.'

'Melons?' Alejandro stared at her.

'I know it sounds stupid.'

He frowned, his eyes probing hers.

Heat flooded her face. 'Cantaloupes, okay. He grabbed them in his hands and said, "These are the most terrific things, like ripe, juicy cantaloupes," and all I could think of was how huge and…fruit-like… I was like a big, chubby berry. Needless to say, it killed my buzz.' She bit down on her lip. 'If it had just been his comment, I might have ignored it, but for years I'd had my mother in my ear, pointing out my many flaws at every opportunity, so whatever confidence I had was shattered into a million tiny pieces.'

He was quiet for so long that she found her eyes lifting to his face. He was very still, his features locked in a mask that she couldn't interpret. 'And you were how old?'

She lifted her shoulders, imitating nonchalance, as though she couldn't remember precisely. 'Seventeen, I think.'

'And he was…?'

'Nineteen.'

Alejandro swore. 'Your breasts are beautiful.' He cupped them gently, reverently, holding them as his eyes drilled into her soul. '*You* are beautiful.' He leaned forward, kissing the tip of her nose, then drifting to her mouth. 'Your hair, your freckles, your eyes, every Irish throwback part of you—whatever cruel lies your mother has fed you over the years, you must know the truth by now.' He teased the side of her lips, then moved his mouth to her shoulder.

'It's just something I accept,' she said after a beat. 'I can't change who I am, so why get upset about it?'

'Are you trying to tell me that you remained a virgin because you didn't feel attractive enough to believe anyone would want you?'

She heard the question, the way he'd distilled her worst fears into a neat little box and placed it between them—a box that was morphing into a bomb, silently ticking, growing closer to detonating.

Oh, great.

Tears sparkled on her lashes. 'You could never understand.'

'That's true. I can't understand. All teenagers go through an awkward phase, but it's fleeting.'

'Are you saying even you were hit by hormones and puberty?'

He dipped his head once in agreement. 'But your mother should have supported you through that, encouraged you.'

'That's not really my mother's style.'

'Olivia?'

'Olivia is a wonderful, supportive older sister.' Her smile, though, was tight. She wanted to break off the conversation, but at the same time her body refused to move. She stayed where she was, feet planted by his, feeling his warmth and nearness and taking comfort from it. 'She has always wanted to fight my battles for me, but we're so different. She loves me but I often think she doesn't understand me.'

'No?'

'She is so poised, so completely in control of her thoughts and feelings—'

'Whereas you say exactly what you think.'

She bit down on her lower lip. 'It's a bad habit of mine.'

'It's one of the things I found irresistible about you, the night we met. You have no artifice, no pretence. You're completely authentic.'

'I think that's called unsophisticated,' she responded with a humorous lilt to her voice.

He caught her chin, lifting her face, surprising her with the dark emotion written across his features. 'Whenever I compliment you, you turn it into a negative. *That* is the only bad habit of yours I am aware of.'

She didn't deny it, nor did she apologise for it. 'It's hard to tune out the internal monologue seeded by my mother. I'm a work in progress.'

Sympathy spiralled through him. 'But she did not attack Olivia?'

'Olivia's life has been far from a walk in the park. Our mother hated her for different reasons.'

'Hate?'

She nodded slowly. 'Olivia is strikingly beautiful in

the same way our mother is—and was. It's been hard for Mum to see Olivia blossoming, to realise that her own beauty is fading with age, while Olivia's is at its zenith.'

But apparently, he wasn't interested in Olivia. 'And you, she treated like an ugly duckling?'

Sienna winced because it was so completely accurate. How could he have understood so perfectly? She nodded once.

'What a fool.'

She lifted her shoulders. 'She has a narrow definition of beauty. I'm nowhere near it.'

'As I said, she is a fool.'

Her lips parted on a rush of hot breath, surprise and something else—it felt as if a part of her was waking, stirring to life. Before she could analyse it further, he was lifting her, carrying her cradled against his chest, down the corridor.

'What are you doing?'

'Isn't it obvious?'

She shook her head, though she had a pretty fair idea.

He shouldered in the bedroom door then placed her down at the edge of the bed. 'You are beautiful. Funny. Smart. Interesting.' He ticked each adjective off on a different finger, enumerating the list in a businesslike way. Nonetheless, each word struck her heart like an arrow, making her stronger, not weakening her. A smile played about her lips and then he was nudging her back onto the bed, his body following hers with the ferocity of a wild animal. His weight pressed to her, his hands pinned hers above her head.

'You deserve to be worshipped so often you never

again doubt the veracity of what I've said. You deserve to be worshipped until you feel like a goddess.'

A shiver ran the length of her body and goosebumps chased after it. But she couldn't respond—there was no time to reply. He kissed her, hard, until her senses were on overload and surrender was the only option. Their coming together was a victory, a victory she felt in every cell of her body, a victory strong enough to rewrite, she suspected, some of her DNA, so that some of the wounds of her adolescence seemed to tremble, to fall away, leaving her with a sense of levity she hadn't known in a long time—if ever.

The desire to protect her was back. Though, of course, it had never left, only subsided a little, with every display of her strength of character and determination. But hearing her describe the relationship with her mother, the way that had shaped her view of herself, made him want to slap the older woman. Oh, he'd never physically hurt a woman, but the anger was the same. How dared she make Sienna feel like this? Wounds that had been inflicted in adolescence were clearly still a part of how Sienna viewed herself, through the lens of her mother's mistreatment.

Anger fired in his body, and a terrifying need to erase her pain. To make her smile for ever. To make it so that she could never again doubt the power of her appeal... But his own past was right there, hovering on the periphery of his mind, the darkness, the hurt, the pain, his inability to protect his mother; all the emotions were jagged edges threatening to enfold him. He pushed them aside, aware they'd never recede completely, but wanting to keep them at bay, at least for now. In this moment, there was pleasure, and they both deserved that.

CHAPTER NINE

SHE FOUND HIM the next morning, early, in the gymnasium. He stood in the centre of the boxing ring, punching the bag hard, rhythmically. Over and over until it shook uncontrollably. He was naked except for a pair of low-slung shorts, so she stood watching in awe of each rippling muscle beneath his bronzed, sheening skin as he moved swiftly, his feet almost dancing every time he repositioned himself.

He punched the bag as though he hated it. As though it were a vile beast and he the only person who could defend humanity against it. Again and again his fists pounded the black leather, his face a study in concentrated rage, and Sienna's awe, at some point, gave way to concern, so she took a step deeper into the room and cleared her throat. He punched the bag once more then dropped his hand, turning to face her, anger lining his eyes and mouth, so he turned away, reached for a towel and wiped his face, as if he wanted to hide the strength of that emotion from her.

She waited, heart pounding, a cascade of emotions rioting through her—admiration at the beauty of his physicality, the strength of his frame and musculature, but also unease, because she'd sensed something within him, something dark and untamed, that made her pulse run wild.

It wasn't that she was afraid. She was fascinated. The same desire to understand him ran through Sienna as he'd claimed to feel the day before. His body was perfection, and it had spent the night making hers soar, sending her into the heavens again and again, but it was also, undeniably, a weapon, capable of inflicting great harm.

She eyed his scars with renewed interest. A beer bottle had caused the one on his chest. But what about the mark on his hip? And the scar on the back of his hand? There was a chink in his nose too, as though it had been broken, possibly more than once.

'A hobby of yours?' She kept her voice light, somehow understanding he wouldn't tolerate her interrogation as well as she had his.

'Exercise.'

She moved closer, breathing in the masculine fragrance of the gym, her eyes locked to his, not looking away. She wasn't afraid of him. In fact, since meeting Alejandro, Sienna had felt emboldened in a new and exciting way—what else explained her decision to fly here and proposition him as she had? That same spirit of strength moved in her now.

'You seem angry.'

'I'm not.' It was clearly a lie.

She eyed the ring thoughtfully, then pushed apart the two middle ropes, stepping into it with her bare feet. She'd taken a moment to pull on one of his shirts, and she was glad, because she wanted to question him without the distraction of too much skin—his near nudity was distracting enough, but the way he looked at *her* made it impossible to think straight.

'I work out most mornings.'

'That explains this.' She lifted a finger, running it over his chest, feeling the ridges there, a sensual smile on her lips. She drifted her finger sideways then, catching the end of his scar, hovering her finger over it, watching him, so she saw the moment his eyes shuttered to her, pushing her away, blocking her out.

She ignored the uncertainty in her gut.

'You said it was a bottle?'

He made a grunting noise of agreement, but didn't move.

'And a drunk?'

This time he tilted his head in what she took to be a tight nod of agreement.

'And so you got good at fighting.'

His lips shifted as though he was grinding his teeth. 'It was necessary.'

'Why?'

His eyes bore into hers and for a moment she thought he wasn't going to answer. And when he spoke, his voice was completely wiped of emotion. 'Because, Sienna, when you live on the streets, being able to defend yourself is not optional.'

Confusion arrowed through her. 'You—went to school with Luca.'

He nodded. 'So?'

'It's a very exclusive school. That's how you met.'

'Yes.'

'And you also lived on the streets?'

He wiped his shoulders with the towel, stepping backwards and dislodging her contact.

But she was filled with curiosity and, suddenly, it was imperative that she know more. 'How do you go from being a street kid to attending a school like that? And why in England? And how did you end up on the streets? What happened to your parents?'

His smile was tight, and she knew he wasn't going to answer. 'So many questions for this time of the morning.'

She wasn't going to be pushed away, though. Part of his building her up the way he had the night before was renewed confidence, and she felt it in her bones. 'I want to understand you.' She threw his words back at him, making it obvious that she was simply going tit for tat.

'There is not much to understand.'

A half-smile curved her lips. 'You're right. Yours sounds like a perfectly typical childhood.'

He walked towards her with a look on his face that didn't invite further questions. His hand lifted to her—his—shirt, undoing the top button, a challenge in his eyes, a look of mockery playing about his lips, as though daring her to continue her line of questioning while he undressed her.

'Will you stay naked today?'

'Will you stay with me if I do?' She hadn't planned to ask that. It hadn't even occurred to her to ask, but she didn't regret the question. It seemed kind of fair.

'No.' His response was just as automatic. 'I can't.' He softened the rejection with a simmering look, and her heart completed an energetic somersault.

Why did he make her feel like the most beautiful

woman in the world? She struggled to think straight when he touched her and, damn it, he knew it. Just the simple act of removing the shirt from her body caused her knees to tremble. Desire stirred in the pit of her stomach. She sank her teeth into her lower lip and when his eyes dropped to the gesture, she knew she was in trouble.

He crooked his finger, pulling her close, and she took the step—just one—with a throbbing, twisting feeling somewhere near her heart.

Their bodies brushed, hers naked, his practically, and she shivered all over now.

'Cold?' But a knowing look glinted in his eyes.

'I—'

Before she could answer, he lifted a hand to her nipple, rolling it between his forefinger and thumb. She felt it harden, felt arrows dart through her, and she tilted her head back, staring at the ceiling as stars flooded her eyes. His touch burned through her, and then his other hand moved between her legs, brushing her sex, so she jerked her face forward, her eyes haunted when they met his.

'You're trying to distract me,' she bit out from beneath clenched teeth, her own hands digging into his shorts, pushing them lower, then removing them until he stood completely naked.

He didn't deny her accusation, simply moved his fingers faster, so she was riding a wave, faster and faster, and she reached for his shoulders, digging her nails into the flesh there, until he brought his head down and kissed her, swallowing her enthusiasm, breathing it in. 'Am I?'

She didn't understand. She was drowning. Pleasure threatened to rip her apart at the seams.

'Alejandro…'

She felt him smile against her mouth, felt his hardness, and sheer longing was a blade in her side. She swore hungrily, pushing at his shoulders, hard, surprising them both, because he stumbled and then she was drawing him to the floor—or perhaps he was leading her, she couldn't tell; Sienna was no longer thinking straight, nor wobbly, she wasn't thinking at all.

He lay on his back and she straddled him, desperate hunger a beast within her.

He went to say something but she kissed him, turning the tables and devouring his words for a change as her body took him deep inside, her muscles tightening around him in eager, grateful welcome. She moved as her instincts dictated, her body's requirements shaping her movements, so she lifted and dropped and groaned as pleasure spun through her, and then Alejandro was moving his body, rolling her onto her back and pulling out of her, so she whimpered at his absence. Then his mouth connected with her sex and all of the pleasure she'd been feeling, all of the build-up, burst in one spectacular hail of stars. She tore her fingers through his hair, lifting her hips as wave after wave of warmth spread through her.

Afterwards, she lay in the centre of the boxing ring, eyes closed, breath rushed, for the several moments it took to pull herself back together, and then to realise that he hadn't experienced the same euphoric release she had. She pushed up onto her elbows, eyes open, one quick glance confirming that he was still rock-hard. She stared at him, confused, and undeniably hurt. It was so easy for her insecurities to creep in, even when he did such an amazing job of making her feel stunning and desirable.

'I— You—'

He moved closer to her, stroking her cheek, his own slashed dark with colour. She stared at him, fascinated, his beauty powerful enough to take her breath away. 'No, I didn't.'

'But—'

She couldn't ask the question that was whispering through her brain. *Didn't you want to?*

She swallowed instead, looked away. Gently, he drew her face back to his.

'I wanted to.' Had he read her mind? How did he know her secret fear? 'But I have never had unprotected sex with a woman, and, no matter how badly I wanted to lose myself in you just now, I will not take that risk.'

She stared at him, not understanding, until the penny finally dropped. She lifted a hand to her mouth, shock making speech, momentarily, impossible.

'I didn't even think—'

'No. You *felt*, and I love how much you feel.' His voice was like a purr, rolling over her skin. 'But I will never lose control in that way, *querida*, no matter how aroused I am.'

'Well, wild horses couldn't have stopped me, so I'm glad you have so much self-control.'

He laughed, unexpectedly. 'That's my job.'

'Why?'

'Because I have more experience with this.'

She considered that. 'So even when I feel as though I'm on the brink of losing my mind, you're still able to function as a rational human?'

His eyes narrowed, and something shifted between them. She couldn't say what, only she sensed a change in him, a tension that made little sense. 'Very slightly rational.'

'That doesn't make me feel any better.'

He kissed her softly. 'It should.' His thumb dragged across her lower lip. 'It just means I respect you enough to take care of you. Neither of us wants an ongoing complication from this.'

He stood up, his body still taut, extending a hand to her, offering her help to stand. She looked up at him, considering that for a moment, but instead she knelt. Her heart was thumping against her ribs so hard she was sure he must be able to hear it, or see it, but his eyes were on her face as she moved closer, her intention obvious to both of them. But would she have the courage to go through with it?

'I've never done this before, so pointers are welcome.' She defused the tension she felt with a joke, then dropped her eyes to his arousal, regarding it for the briefest second before she moved her tongue over his tip, slowly at first, then down his entire length, tasting him before she took him deep in her mouth, relishing the feeling of him there, and even more so when he let out a loud, primal groan that seemed to reverberate against the gym's walls. His body trembled as she moved her mouth, and his hands on her shoulders were gentle, as if he needed her support.

Fierce heat travelled her body, the strength of his desire was an aphrodisiac she hadn't expected, so she found she never wanted this to end, she never wanted to stop. Power exploded through her, and when he lost himself, she felt a part of herself go right along with him, as though they were bound together in an inexplicable, undeniable way.

Was it any wonder Alejandro couldn't concentrate? Whenever he got five minutes to himself, he found his mind replaying, over and over, their morning, and a flood of desire ravaged his body, making it impossible to think, to work, to do anything but pace, his blood as hot as lava.

He'd woken so angry! Furious, in fact. The dark emotions had pounded through him in a way he hadn't experienced since childhood. As a little boy, he'd always felt that anger, his impotence, his inability to fix his mother's life. He'd felt defensive and protective, and yet there'd been nothing he could do for her, nothing he could do to save her. Every time a strange man had come to their tiny apartment and she'd taken him into her room, Alejandro had worried. He'd seen her hurt enough times, seen her with black eyes and bloody noses, and he'd been terrified that she would die. Then one day she did, and instead of feeling guilty he'd felt numb, because he'd always known her life would end that way.

Why, after so many years of detachment, had those protective instincts kicked in all over again, and for Sienna Thornton-Rose?

Because of her eyes.

He closed his own, pressing his hands to his hips as his body faced towards the windows of his office.

Her eyes told him so much, and when she'd spoken of her adolescence, casually referring to the way her mother had treated her, insulted and belittled her, and her unpleasant experiences with flirtation and sex in the past, he'd seen the pain in her features, he'd seen the insecurities that still dogged her, and he'd wanted to stop the world from spinning and fundamentally re-shape it. How a vibrant, funny, beautiful young woman like Sienna could ever think she wasn't enough of any-thing was practically a criminal offence.

It wasn't just the things she'd said, though. He'd felt the same kick of protectiveness when he'd seen her at the wedding in Rome, when he'd heard the way her mother had spoken to her about her hair, when he'd seen her look of compliance and acceptance, he'd felt a pow-erful rush of anger, a need to replace all that hurt with something else, something warm and pleasurable. He'd wanted her, but he'd also wanted to fix things for her.

He'd woken angry this morning, and sought refuge in his gym, with a workout that had been so intense he could feel each and every muscle screaming now, but he barely even noticed that. He could think only of Sienna as she'd been in the gym, how she'd looked at him, how she'd taken control and ridden him as though her life depended on it. But most of all, he thought about how goddamned hard he'd found it to stop what they were doing, how tempted he'd been to lose himself in her regardless of the consequences. It was a temptation he'd *never* known before, not with any other woman.

'Control' might as well have been his middle name. He didn't lose his head, he didn't lose his mind, and he never lost sight of his rules. But with Sienna, everything had an urgency that was new. He'd wanted her to the point that he could hardly even care what would happen if she fell pregnant.

And that had scared the living hell out of him.

It still did, if he was honest.

What he needed was to change gears, just until he could rediscover his equilibrium with her, to regain control. In his home, all he could think of was stripping her naked and exploring her body, and for the first time in his life he could appreciate the difficulty separating sex from emotions. He didn't *feel*, because he had trained himself not to, but with Sienna, he saw risk—not only for himself, but for her too, and he intended to avoid those risks at all costs.

The problem was, everything with her was *different*. The way they'd met: she was the first woman he'd ever been asked to spend time with. The first woman he'd ever been prohibited from sleeping with. The first virgin he'd had sex with. She was also the first woman who'd propositioned him in such a cavalier manner, and the first woman he'd invited into his home. What he needed was to make things between them more normal. To make her like any of the women he usually slept with, to make their relationship more familiar, and less unique. Familiar equated to forgettable and at the end of all this, he needed to be able to forget Sienna. He suspected a lot in his life depended on that—including his friendship with Luca and, likely, his equilibrium.

* * *

Let's eat out tonight.

Sienna couldn't believe that even a simple four-word text message from Alejandro could stir her blood to fever pitch, but the sight of his name on her screen sparked an instant reaction within her.

She let herself imagine what that would be like, but reality was right there, wrapping around her, even if he'd momentarily forgotten a major part of their agreement.

Tempting, but not possible.

Why not?

Because this is supposed to be our little secret, and you're Alejandro Corderó. You get noticed wherever you go.

Not everywhere.

Curiosity sparked in her blood.

No?

No.

Her heart sped up, but still doubts plagued her.

I don't want Olivia and Luca to find out about this.

Three dots appeared to show that he was typing, then they disappeared, only to reappear a moment later.

Trust me.

Her heart skipped a couple of beats. She looked towards the pool, shimmering in the early evening light. *Trust me. Trust me.* Did she trust him? And if so, why? Trust wasn't something she handed out to just anyone, but the more she thought about it, the more she relaxed, the more she smiled.

Will I need a disguise?

Like a secret agent?

She grinned.

Exactly.

The idea of you wearing a trench coat with nothing underneath holds definite appeal.

She was too turned on to reply. She put her phone down and strolled inside his beautiful home, a smile beaming from her face. Retrieving a drink from the kitchen, she moved back to the deck, and saw he'd sent one last text.

I'll pick you up at eight.

Her heart fluttered with anticipation.

It's a date.

Except, she reminded herself, it wasn't. Not in the ordinary sense. This was…well, she didn't know exactly, but not that. And it didn't matter.

She was enjoying herself. She was learning about men and sex and how great it could feel. She was doing something purely for herself, and she wasn't going to overthink it. She was just going to let go and enjoy the ride, in the full knowledge that soon it would be over, and normal programming would resume.

CHAPTER TEN

JUST BEFORE FIVE o'clock that evening, there was a buzzing sound, and she moved towards it with a perplexed expression.

'Delivery.'

She pulled open the door, bemused to find the concierge there, holding a bag towards her.

She took it, closing the door with a thundering heart, peering inside only once she was deep into the lounge room again.

And a smile lifted her lips, at the same time uncertainty dipped her heart.

'Leather pants?' She squeaked, pulling them so a piece of paper dropped to the floor. She scooped it up, saw his handwriting confident and bold.

Trust me. A

She put the paper down and turned her attention back to the pants, remembering their earlier conversation when he'd joked about wanting to see her in a pair. But it was madness. Sienna had never worn anything so figure-hugging. She *couldn't*.

So why did her fingers curl around the supple material and lift it higher, towards her chest? Why did she clutch them as she moved into the bathroom?

They fitted like a glove, and when she spun around and peered over her shoulder, into the mirror, she wasn't completely disgusted by what she saw.

She couldn't have said what she expected for their not-really-a-date, but when she stepped into the luxury foyer a few hours later, it was to find Alejandro already there, his eyes pinned to the elevator with an intensity that stole her breath. It was as though he'd been waiting for her all his life, not simply for a few minutes. She tried to modulate her breathing, but it was rushing out of her in fits and spurts, and the closer she got, the worse it felt.

He moved his finger in a semi-circle pattern. 'Let me see.'

Her heart leaped to her throat as she did as he said, and began to twirl, slowly.

The low, guttural noise of appreciation was a salve she hadn't known she needed.

'Almost perfect.'

'Almost?'

He reached into his pocket, removing a small black velvet pouch. She took it without thinking, expecting it to contain something irrelevant, something small and trivial, so she flicked it open and upended it over her palm, only to find a stunning green gem on a fine rose-gold chain. The emerald was raw, not super polished, making it look almost as if it were alive—patches of pale green, vivid green and black swirled together beneath a slightly porous exterior. She stared at it, the beauty unmistakable, a lump in her throat making speech difficult.

'It's lovely.' What an insipid word. 'What's it for?'

'It is for you.' A simple answer that told her nothing.

'Why?'

'Why not?'

Her heart stammered. Was this what he did on dates? How he made his lovers feel special?

Everything slowed down as sense gradually replaced wonderment. Of course it was. This was an act. He did this all the time. It was only her inexperience that made it all seem so special. He was treating her as he would any of his other lovers. It wasn't special. It wasn't unique. It didn't mean anything.

'You don't need to buy me gifts,' she blurted out, the gesture strangely tainted by her knowledge that this was him going through the motions.

'I know that.' He took it from her and reached behind her neck, clasping the necklace in place, then leaning back just far enough to admire it. He shifted his head in a small nod of approval.

'Are you ready?'

Could she ever be? 'Where are we going?'

'You'll see.'

As they approached the doors of the foyer the concierge swished them open and they stepped into the balmy night air, the smell of the sea wrapping around them, so she inhaled deeply, without thinking, the romance of that aroma sweeping her away. She was too distracted to notice the bike at first, too overwhelmed by the way he looked in a navy-blue suit, but when he began to unpin her hair, pulling to loosen it, she gasped at the intimacy and how, on some level, she'd simply known he would do that.

'You don't like it in a bun?'

'I like it fine.' His voice was low and gravelled. 'But this wouldn't fit.'

And he reached behind them, grabbing a shining black helmet off a motorbike, and easing it over her head, so the world faded, like a tinted version of itself.

'A disguise?'

'Safety,' he responded, but with a curl of his lips that showed appreciation for her joke.

He reached for her hand, guiding her towards the bike. 'Have you ever ridden before?'

She shook her head. 'Never.'

'We seem to enjoy sharing your firsts together.'

Heat flushed her body. 'You ride?' She took a moment to appraise the bike, moving around it, admiring the shape of it, the size, thinking that it reminded her of a crouched bull, with barely contained strength indicated by the sculpted metal.

'My first car was a bike.' He cast one powerful leg over the frame, then shot her a look—a dare. 'Hop on.'

A frisson of anticipation warmed her as she did exactly that, taking up the space behind him, her legs hugging his frame. When he started the bike, she leaned forward, wrapping her arms around him, and pressure built behind her ribs, like the gathering of an electrical storm. She felt its charge and its strength and relished the possession of both.

The bike throbbed beneath them, and the storm grew in intensity, so her hands were no longer content to stay as they were, neatly folded over his chest. They explored, stroking his body, his ribs, his muscles, feeling him as the bike seemed to take on the personality of an animal, tearing them through Barcelona. She was aware of the city as he drove, of the changing landscape, from the cultured, exquisite frontages of the Passeig de Gràcia to the slightly grittier feel of the next neighbourhood, with art almost everywhere she looked—on the sides of buildings, billboards, even the street had been painted at the edges, passing her by in a blur until Alejandro stopped at the lights.

Idling, the bike's rhythm stirred her to fever pitch, so she shifted closer on the seat, pressing her legs into him more tightly, until his hand reached down and stroked her thigh, and pleasure burst through her.

He navigated the streets expertly, as though he were wired for them, turning the bike away from a busy road down a side street and then another, with little restaurants dotted between shops and galleries, until finally he drew to a stop right out at the front of a string of three restaurants. It had taken less than ten minutes in all—not long enough. She wanted more. The thrill of being behind him as he expertly drove them through Barcelona had been immense.

'Enjoy yourself?' he asked as she stepped off the bike.

Sienna struggled to catch her breath. 'Yes.' What was the point in lying? She unhooked the helmet—heavier than she'd expected—and held it out to him. 'I liked it a lot.'

His grin showed that he knew, or perhaps that he'd expected. 'I thought you might.' He leaned closer. 'Daredevil.'

She blinked up at him, the moniker not one that had ever been used to describe her, and yet she liked it, and she couldn't entirely argue with it. Since meeting Alejandro, she felt as though all she'd done was take risks—and they'd paid off, big time.

'Where are we?'

'El Born.' He secured the helmets on the handlebar, then took her hand automatically—strange how comfortable that felt—as he strode towards a bright red door with ornate lampposts on either side. Sienna looked up and down the street, noting the small details now—the cobbled road that weaved between the buildings, the terracotta finish of the walls, the church at the end that seemed to have all rounded walls, and then the noise of the restaurants, the chatter and song that overflowed with happiness.

'This is a medieval part of town,' he explained, opening the door for her. The noise grew instantly louder. He stepped in behind her, shutting the door, so they were alone on a small landing. He gestured towards the stairs—too narrow for them to walk side by side. In fact, as she made her way down the stairs, Sienna had to dip her head a little, owing to the low roof.

It opened up once she reached the bottom. The room seemed to grow out of nowhere, stone walls covered in shelves and bottles, plants with long tendrils scrambling wildly across the space, the room dark except for the occasional lamp casting a golden glow, so there was privacy and anonymity in every direction. Towards the back of the restaurant, couples were dancing, their movements unmistakably traditional Spanish, mysterious and beautiful, and so elegant Sienna ached to be able to move just like them.

A waitress greeted them above the noise, and Alejandro switched to Catalan, so Sienna didn't catch what he asked, only a moment later they were shown to a table near the front of the restaurant, a jug of sangria brought almost immediately.

'It's tradition.' He grinned, gesturing to the jug.

She eyed it thoughtfully. 'Another first for me.'

'You cannot be serious?'

'Tell me when in my life you think I might have had the opportunity to drink sangria,' she prompted, pouring two glasses and looking at it curiously.

'You've never been to Spain?'

'I've barely been anywhere,' she corrected. 'In fact, until Olivia's vows in Rome, my passport had been lapsed for about a decade.'

He leaned closer. 'Because money was so tight?'

'Yes. Travelling was the last thing on any of our minds.' She sipped the drink, relishing the flavours. 'It tastes like summer.'

'As it's supposed to.'

'I was thinking, the other day, how money can open the world up to you. I would never have been able to come to Barcelona to see you, before…'

'Olivia's marriage to Luca,' he prompted.

'Right. It's only that some of my father's inheritance has been freed up that we have that liberty now.'

'What about your job? It doesn't involve travel?'

'No. In fact, I work from home. It's the only way.'

'Why?'

She traced her finger around the rim of the glass.

'My mother didn't want Olivia or me to leave,' she admitted. 'And we didn't feel that we could. She might seem like an awful person, and in so many ways she is, but at the same time she's my mother, and I do love her, Alejandro. More than that, I pity her. She's a product of my father's monstrous behaviour. I've got enough perspective to see that she's spent my entire life projecting her own insecurities onto me.'

He was watching her through hooded eyes, seeing too much and revealing nothing.

'Anyway...' She sucked in a breath, eager to move the conversation on. 'Travel wasn't really a big priority. Until it was.'

He leaned closer, and beneath the table their knees brushed, reminding her of the leather trousers she wore, the trousers he'd bought for her.

'These are the perfect size, by the way.'

He didn't miss a beat. 'It's almost like I remember every delectable inch of your body.'

Her stomach flipped.

'Well enough to describe it to a sales assistant.'

'I hope not.' She looked away, heat flaming her face.

He laughed softly.

'So is this all part of your usual modus operandi?' She took a larger gulp of her drink.

'What, in particular?'

'Buying women clothes, jewels, making them feel as though they are the only woman on earth for a night.'

He straightened. 'Is that what I've done?'

Her heart seemed to tighten. He was surprised. No, he was scared, as though she'd suggested he might be about to propose marriage. Damn her straight talking! Damn her inability to think anything through.

'I'm only joking,' she lied, rolling her eyes for good measure. 'I'm just asking what the norm is for you. When you date women.'

'I don't date, remember?'

Something jolted in her chest. 'You know what I mean. I've seen photos of you with women, at events.'

'Sure. As a prelude to sex, nothing more.'

Her stomach turned. She felt hot and cold, and not in a good way. Panic set in, so she reached for her drink once more, sipping it slowly, to buy time, hoping she looked more relaxed than she felt. Why did such a cold assessment of his nocturnal activities make something in her belly spin out of control?

The waitress reappeared to take their order, and Sienna sat back while Alejandro spoke, listing a selection of dishes that she could partially understand.

When they were alone again, she felt a little more clear-headed; her heart—so used to being battered— had recovered as it always did.

'Why don't you date?' she asked directly, curiosity sparking too large to ignore now.

'What's the point?'

She flexed one brow, waiting for him to elaborate.

'Isn't dating the route you take to marriage? Why bother, given that I don't intend to get married?'

'I think you're being too binary in your thinking,' she said after a moment. 'After all, I intend to get married, but not to fall in love. I intend to date to find a suitable husband, not to fall in love.'

'And will you tell your husband how limited you want your marriage to be?'

A cheeky smile flickered on her lips. 'Do you think me capable of lying?'

'Not for one moment.'

She sighed with assumed melodrama. 'Then what choice do I have?'

If he was amused by her comment, he didn't show it. 'And what sort of man do you think you'll find, who's willing to marry you in name only?'

'Oh, I don't mean for the marriage to be in name only, necessarily.'

'What does that mean?'

She lifted her shoulders. 'I'm not getting married with the intention of getting divorced again right away.'

'But to satisfy your father's will, you need only to marry, correct?'

'Yes. But the idea of doing it *just* to meet his dictatorial requirements doesn't sit right with me. I'd prefer to find someone I actually like, someone I can be friends with, and forge a relationship with them.'

'And will sex form a part of this relationship?'

Something like nausea wretched through her. The idea of another man touching her, kissing her, making love to her, was like swallowing acid. 'Undoubtedly,' she said, reaching for her drink only to realise it was empty. Alejandro didn't take his eyes off her face as he lifted the jug, refilling her glass.

'Be careful, *querida*. It tastes sweet but it packs a punch.'

She sipped it defiantly. 'I don't want to live a sexless life, if that's what you're asking. Nor do I want to cheat on my husband. So I suppose I'll have to find someone I find sexually attractive as well.'

But the idea made her head swim, because that had never been part of her plan. Alejandro had set the cat amongst the pigeons, showing her body what it could feel, making her crave him around the clock, so she couldn't imagine going on with her life without that kind of satisfaction.

'Perhaps Tinder?'

Was she imagining the dark edge to his words? Probably. Wishful thinking. Why would he care what she planned to do with her life?

Tapas began to appear at their table, a selection of crumbed olives, anchovies on toast, saffron-flavoured rice balls, and vegetables in olive oil. Sienna ate, grateful Alejandro moved the conversation on to something more general, entertaining her with the history of this area of Barcelona, while Sienna went through the motions, eating though she was no longer hungry, praising the food though she could barely taste it.

She was surprised to realise, when all the plates were cleared, that almost two hours had passed, and the sangria jug was almost empty. She hadn't seen him take more than a couple of sips from his glass, so she suspected she'd had rather too much to drink. Whoops.

When they stood, she did indeed feel a little woozy, but the hand he put in the small of her back anchored her back to this room, this restaurant, to him, so she moved her body close to his, closing her eyes as she inhaled his intoxicating, masculine fragrance.

'Would you like to dance, *querida*?'

'Don't you remember? I have two left feet.'

'It doesn't matter. You'll feel the music.' He stroked her arm. 'Trust me.'

Something stirred low in her abdomen, spreading through her whole body, and when she looked up into his eyes, she was lost. *Trust me.* Why did that sound like both a spell and a curse at the same time?

CHAPTER ELEVEN

THE NEXT TIME he stopped the motorbike it was not at the base of his penthouse, but in a small, crowded area with buildings so close they were like teeth in an overcrowded mouth. Alejandro cut the engine but didn't speak for a moment, so she looked around, watching as a guy slowly approached the window of an idling car.

Two women dressed in revealing outfits watched from across the narrow street.

'Where are we?'

Her question seemed to rouse him. 'My past.'

Curiosity sparked. 'Oh?'

'Let me show you something.'

Anything. She caught the word just in time, proud of herself for finally not saying the first thing that popped into her head. He secured the helmets then laced his fingers through hers, pulling her close to his side. She loved the way it felt there. Just right. They fitted together as though they'd been designed—somehow, she caught the thought before it could go any further, terminating it and turning to him with a bright smile. 'I can smell the sea.'

'It's not far from here.'

'Did you go swimming much as a child? Play pirates at the seashore?'

Her tone was light, but when she glanced up at his face, she stopped walking. There was a tension there that broke her heart. 'Alejandro? What is it?'

He seemed to rouse himself, turning to face her. 'I haven't been back here in a long time.'

Her brows drew together. 'Then why—?'

'You said you want to understand me.'

She nodded slowly, a tic in her heart making her aware that it was moving too fast. 'But not if it's hurting you to show me.'

Surprise flashed in his eyes. He looked away. A cat scampered across the footpath in front of them, jet black, barely discernible for how dark the street was. Alejandro wrapped his arm around her shoulders, holding her closer, leading her further up the street. It was quiet—no signs of nightlife, but they weren't alone. There were more scantily clad women lined up against the walls, and the men she saw looked as though they were out of it. A sense of danger prickled along her skin, but when she was with Alejandro, she felt safe. Completely and utterly.

'This is where I spent the first twelve years of my life. In this tenement, two small rooms—a kitchen and sofa in one, a bedroom in the other. I slept on the sofa. There was a shared bathroom, used by everyone on our floor.'

Sympathy filled Sienna's eyes. She wrapped her arm around his waist, running her fingers over his side, and she waited. He'd brought her here after all. It wasn't to block her questions.

'The area has been cleaned up considerably since then, believe it or not.' They looked in unison towards a car that was drawing to a stop near the women. One approached the window, spoke for a moment, then came around to the front passenger side. She stepped in, and the car drove down the street.

'If this is "cleaned up", what was it like when you were a boy?'

'Gangs ran everything. The streets were filled with drugs and prostitutes, brothels in every building.' He started to walk, drawing her with him. 'My mother fought so hard, she wanted to get away from it all. She got a job working as a waitress, but once she had me, with no support, her options dried up—she turned to prostitution because she could not see another choice. Her life had not been easy—she'd grown up rough, so coming back here, falling in with the gangs, it must have seemed like her only option. She worked out of our apartment.'

Sienna gasped. She had gathered that he was 'self-made' from the research she'd done, but she hadn't imagined his start in life to be quite so tough as this.

'The gang she worked for controlled her life. Who she saw, what she did. She was only sixteen when I was born.'

Sienna gasped again. 'Oh, Alejandro.' It was no longer enough to stand with her arm around his waist. She moved to the front of him, wrapping both arms behind his back, lifting up onto the tips of her toes and kissing the base of his throat. 'I'm so sorry.'

'It's a long time ago now.'

'You said you lived here until you were twelve,' she

said quietly after a moment, trying not to cry, but her mouth was filling with the sting of tears and her eyes hurt like hell. 'What happened? Where did you go after that?'

His lips curled in a derisive half-smile, and then it fell, leaving his expression empty, blanked, a mask of determination that couldn't quite hide all his pain. 'The streets. My mother died. If I wanted to continue living in the apartment—paid for by the gang who'd used her—I had to agree to work for them. If there was one thing I'd learned growing up and seeing the way my mother was treated, it was that nobody was going to have that kind of control over my life. I would not work for anyone. I would not live in fear of anyone.'

Sienna couldn't stop a tear from rolling down her cheek, but she angled her face away, knowing he wouldn't want her sympathy even as it was pouring out of her.

'I moved to the city centre. I stole food. I lived rough. I learned to fight. I grew up damned fast.' His laugh was hoarse, as though his throat were lined with acid. Sienna closed her eyes, shivering to imagine a young boy, only twelve, living that kind of life. Now he turned to face her, looking into her eyes, and what she saw in his expression made her heart thump to a stop. He was still that twelve-year-old boy—fully grown now, but his experiences haunted him, dogged him, and turned him into the man he was today. Uber-successful, determined, but alone. No emotional commitments, he wasn't close to anyone. Except Luca.

And now she was making him lie to his best friend. A hint of guilt stole through her, because she was a grown woman and shouldn't have felt the need to hide the truth from her brother-in-law, but, damn it, she wanted this experience to be hers, just hers. Nobody else needed to know. It wasn't as if he had any reason to share the details of this relationship, anyway. He wasn't the kind of man who'd fill anyone in—even Luca—on the intricacies of his personal life.

'Why the city?'

'Better protection, fewer gangs.'

'You must have been terrified.'

He fixed her with a steely gaze, but she felt everything he was trying to conceal behind a mask of strength. 'It wasn't as though life with my mother was a peach.'

'No?' she whispered, but she didn't need him to elaborate. She could imagine.

'She was treated like dirt. I saw. I heard. I knew.'

His hand had formed a fist at his side; she reached down, curving hers over it, wishing there were some way she could erase that trauma for him. 'You must have hated it.'

He didn't respond. She ached for him, and for his mother. 'Is that how she died?'

His lips tightened. 'Occupational hazard,' he said after a beat. 'I couldn't save her. I tried.'

Pain ripped through Sienna. She lifted her other hand to his chest, placing it over his heart. She heard his guilt, the failure, the regret. She wanted to obliterate those emotions and memories from his mind. 'I am so sorry you had to live through that.'

He shrugged with assumed nonchalance. 'Others had it worse.'

Perhaps, but not by much.

He caught her hand again, guiding her through the ancient laneways. She shivered involuntarily. What had, at first, seemed like a rabbit warren of streets—ancient and fascinating, albeit rundown—was now subsumed by darkness for Sienna. She could feel only his pain, imagine him as an adolescent, alone and terrified, and she wanted to hug him close and reassure him that he'd never know that pain again.

A chasm seemed to form in her chest, a hole right near her heart. She squeezed his hand, struggling to find any words. They walked past the bike, a little further down the street, to a small green park with a statue of Mary and Jesus in the centre. 'She used to come and pray here, to ask God to deliver her to a better life. I would hear her words and wonder when He would answer.'

Tears slid down Sienna's cheeks; she angled her face towards the street and wiped them away surreptitiously. 'When I bought my first company, and I had more money than I knew what to do with, I made it my mission to answer my mother's prayers. It was too late for her, but not for all the women out there living as she did, who wanted help, who were brave enough to ask for it.'

Now she looked up at him, uncaring that he would see the moisture in her eyes. 'How?'

'In a very similar way to how you plan to help, actually.'

She didn't immediately understand.

'I own hundreds of apartments across Spain. I work with a charity to rent them to women who are in need. Single mothers, predominantly. The rent is affordable, or free, depending on circumstance. It is a small thing, to help them get on their feet, to escape lives in which they might otherwise be trapped.'

Her throat was too thick to allow speech. Her heart was overflowing. It was such a quiet, pragmatic, unassuming way to help. 'I didn't know.'

'Why would you?'

'I work in the charity sector, and I read a few articles about you before I came here. I'm surprised it's not mentioned.'

'I don't make it publicly known. The ownership of the apartments is at arm's length to me. I don't need to advertise what I'm doing.'

It was, if anything, the icing on the cake. To help for the sake of helping, rather than for plaudits and praise. 'Your mother would be very proud of you.'

'I wish there'd been someone who could have helped her.'

'You wish *you* could have helped her,' she said gently, lifting her hand and cupping his cheek.

'Of course. But I was a child. The one time I tried, it only made it worse.'

Her heart splintered apart for him.

'After that, she begged me not to get involved. She gave me headphones and a Discman, made me sit in the lounge room and listen to music.'

'But you didn't.'

A muscle jerked at the base of his jaw and she knew that she was right.

She leaned forward and pressed a kiss to his chest. She felt him still, and was afraid to look up, afraid to meet his eyes, because something was building inside her, a feeling that was growing and bursting, a feeling that terrified her. A feeling she couldn't understand but that she knew she needed to run from. 'Let's go back now, Alejandro. This isn't your life anymore.'

She was wrong. It would always be his life. He had grown up, but never away, from that life, those nights, those feelings.

He watched her sleeping, fascinated by the gentle undulations of her breasts, the subtle rise and fall of her creamy skin, the fire-engine red of her hair, the parting of her full, lush lips, the fluttering of her eyelids and the shifting of her thick, dark lashes. He watched her sleep but he felt the weight of his past and failure, the heavy ache of his own inability to save his mother, to remove her from that situation, when he'd had the skills all along. True, he'd been younger, but after she'd died, and he'd made his way in the world, he'd been better off than when they'd lived in that apartment. If only he'd made her leave sooner, made her run away from that life, those obligations.

She'd been so young, still a child herself in many ways. She'd had no one to fight for her.

He couldn't help it. Despite the fact Sienna slept so peacefully—that she was exhausted—he reached out and brushed his finger over her cheek, lightly, just because he needed to feel her and to know that she was real, that she was here. Attempting to slot her into the box other women had occupied in his life had failed. She wasn't like them, and nor was this affair.

She anchored him in a way he'd never known before. Having her here changed his apartment in some vital way, as though it had become an actual 'home', and not just a place to sleep, and he couldn't put his finger on how or why she'd done that, but he knew that he liked it.

And that was, in and of itself, a danger.

Because Alejandro didn't want to get used to the comfort she offered. He didn't want to soften the edges his life had carved into hard planes. He didn't want to forget that he was alone, that he couldn't rely on anyone, that he didn't want to carry the burden of someone else's happiness and protection lest he fail all over again. He could never forgive himself for the ways in which he'd let down his mother. The thought of doing so again—and to someone like Sienna—was impossible to contemplate.

He'd taken her to dinner in an attempt to get them out of the bedroom, to stall the emotional intimacy that had been luring them closer, dangerously close, and because he'd wanted to lighten the mood between them, but the ploy had failed. And because of him. *He* was the one who'd taken her to the streets he'd grown up in, given her a necklace and shown her more of his true self than he ever had another soul. He'd aimed to push her away a little and instead he'd shown her a part of him that he usually kept locked away.

And he had no idea why, but he did know he had to get a grip on the situation, before things went any further. He stood abruptly and strode from the room, from Sienna, simply to prove to himself that he still could.

Across the Balearic Sea, in Rome, Luca stared at the photograph with a flush of fever-like heat. Alejandro he'd recognise anywhere, and his face was towards the camera when the picture was snapped. The woman he was dancing with was less discernible, given that her back was turned, her face only very slightly in profile. But her skin was pale and her hair flame red, and there was something in the way she had been photographed moving that drove a stake through his chest, because he knew instantly who it was.

What was less clear was how in the world his wife's sister had been photographed dancing in a tapas bar in Barcelona with Luca's best friend. The picture, poor quality so presumably taken from a cell phone by an opportunistic diner who saw a chance to make a quick buck by on-selling the image to the tabloids, was nothing new—Alejandro was photographed at events often. But with Sienna?

Years of friendship and goodwill lived in Luca, but for a moment there was rage too, because he'd trusted Alejandro, and the idea of Sienna being tossed aside after a brief fling—which was the only way Alejandro knew how to treat women—made Luca's blood boil. He'd asked the man to *protect* her, not to treat her like any of his other lovers. Alejandro was incapable of genuine emotion with women, incapable of commitment— there was no other conclusion but that he was flirting with Sienna for fun. And she stood to get hurt if she believed, for even one second, that Alejandro was boyfriend material. Everything he knew about Sienna had come from Olivia. He knew how sheltered she'd been, how protected, how badly bullied by their mother, how that had impacted her self-esteem. He also knew that she had no experience with men, particularly not a man like Alejandro who saw sex as the scratching of a physical itch and nothing more.

He closed the paper hurriedly as Olivia entered the kitchen.

'Everything okay, *caro*?'

'Hmm? Oh, yes. Of course.'

And it would be—just as soon as he'd seen Alejandro and got an explanation as to what the hell was going on.

CHAPTER TWELVE

She was conscious of the sun streaming through her window, she was conscious of Alejandro dressing, but she didn't move. She lay there, eyes closed, feigning sleep, because she wasn't ready to face him yet.

They had one more night together. It didn't feel like enough, even when it was what they'd agreed.

Which was all the more reason for her to get the heck out of there. Since she'd first learned of her father's will, Sienna had formed a clear plan for her life, and it included a safe, sensible marriage. Definitely not this.

Not sex she craved as though it were an essential part of life, not a heart that was falling head over heels for someone—someone who could hurt her, just as her dad had hurt her mother. She was smarter than that—she'd learned the lessons her mother had refused to heed.

And she was no coward. She blinked her eyes open, sitting up, forcing herself to meet his gaze and smile, even when all her good resolutions felt as though they might evaporate in response to the steam that came off his appraisal.

Belatedly, she realised the sheet was wrapped around

her waist and she wore the flimsiest of camisoles, barely covering her breasts. 'Good morning.'

He finished buttoning his shirt then strode towards her. Sienna's body lurched; everything felt off kilter.

'Hi.' He sat on the edge of the bed, one strong arm over her legs, his face closer to hers. 'How did you sleep?'

Tortured by dreams of him.

'Fine.' She cleared her throat. 'You?'

His smile showed so much. That he understood what she hadn't said…that he felt it deep within him as well.

'Barely.' He leaned forward, pressing a kiss against her lips, lingering there, so she shifted slightly, pressing her body forward.

His laugh was a soft caress, then he stood, his absence like ice water, dousing her, outraging her. She said nothing.

'We'll go out again tonight. I'll text you details.'

'It could be more fun to stay in,' she said with the hint of a pout about her lips.

He simply smiled, dismissively, so frustration bubbled through her. But perhaps it *was* smarter to go out. Here there was nothing to do but discover one another, to make love and talk and kiss and learn, and she was afraid walking away without a backwards glance would be a lot harder if they kept going down that road.

'See you later.'

A hint of defiance ran through Sienna as she shopped for something to wear that night. It was their last night together, and though she felt her usual desire to downplay her curves, she ignored it, instead opting to try on dresses that emphasised her figure—a stunning cock-tail gown with a low-cut neckline, spaghetti straps and a knee-length skirt clung to her body like a second skin, hiding nothing. She was terrified of that, but she'd also seen the way Alejandro looked at her, she knew that when he looked at her body he didn't see the pinchable sides of her stomach or the roundedness of her butt—at least, he didn't see those things in a negative way. She paid for the dress before she could change her mind, then selected some strappy slingbacks. On a whim, she stopped off at a salon near his apartment, getting her hair trimmed and blown out so it hung in loose, volu-minous curls around her face.

Excitement built as the day passed, and finally, just after seven, she showered, careful not to dampen her hair, then dressed, nervousness almost making her change out of the revealing outfit and opt for one of her more conservative dresses.

But time was marching on, and she wanted to be waiting for him when he arrived.

Her heart hammered with anticipation and when her phone began to hum, she lifted it up, a smile on her face.

'I'm downstairs.'

Her breath throbbed. 'Okay. I'll see you soon.'

Her heart was racing, her blood firing through her veins, and now she forced herself to do one last check in the mirror. And swore under her breath. Because smiling back at Sienna was a woman who seemed as though she had the world in the palm of her hand. She looked confident and even a little sophisticated. Except for her hands, which trembled as they reached for her clutch bag. She placed it between her side and her arm and stepped into the lift, adrenaline turning her body in a highly charged electrical current.

The lift sailed downwards, and when the doors pinged open it took precisely two seconds for her to locate Alejandro. He was waiting a short distance away, and when their eyes met, time stood still. He stared at her, and she stared right back, a thousand feelings exploding through her, until the lift doors began to close, and she startled, moving her hand between them so they sprang apart once more. But in that split second of inaction, Alejandro was moving, his whole body sliding between the doors and propelling her backwards, dwarfing her and pinning her at the same time, pressing her to the back of the elevator as his mouth sought hers and his hand moved to the panel, pressing buttons without lifting his face from hers.

She whimpered into the kiss, the ache that had been building inside her all day, needing this and him so badly it hurt, both mollified and intensified by the power of his kiss, and without realising what she was doing she lifted one leg, straining the stretchy material of the dress—but she didn't care. She curved her leg behind him, holding him close, and she kissed him as though her very life depended upon it.

He swore, the kind of curse she loved hearing on his lips because it evoked the sea and salt and flavour of this wild, ancient, primal city; she loved it because it spoke of desperation and need, and a fever coursing through his body the way it was hers. The elevator moved upwards and she pulled away just long enough to say, 'What happened to dinner?'

His answer was to lift her over his shoulder and

stride out of the lift the second the doors opened. Once in his apartment, he placed her down in the middle of the room, sliding her body along his, and though she wanted, more than anything, for him to kiss her again, there was something in the way he looked at her that made her blood spark like lava. He took a step back, one hand still latched to hers, his eyes slipping from her eyes to her lips, lower to the swell of generous cleavage revealed by her dress, to her pinched-in waist and then the curve of her hips, her legs, until she could hardly stand it a second longer.

'Dinner?' she prompted with an arched brow.

'Screw dinner.' Then he was moving forward, kissing her all over again, undressing her as he moved them backwards, towards the chaise of the sofa, tumbling them backwards, his hands removing the dress she'd so daringly chosen, his groan cutting through time and space when he realised she wasn't wearing a bra beneath it. His hands fondled her breasts, his body pressed down on hers, as she undressed him with the same desperate hunger as he displayed with her, until they were both naked, writhing, tangled together, a war of passion and possession breaking around them, splintering the world apart, so Sienna was conscious of nothing but Alejandro, and him she was aware of on a cellular level. His breath across her skin, the weight of his body, the warmth of his flesh, the vapour on his skin, the smell of his cologne, the taste of his mouth.

'You are—' but he didn't finish the sentence; he couldn't. Instead, he drove himself into her, pinning her arms above her head, staring right into her eyes as he moved, thrusting deep and fast at first, then slowly, and the look in his eyes, for the briefest moment, drove passion from Sienna's mind, because he was lost, and looking at her as though salvation might be found within her.

She pushed up onto her elbows, dislodging his grip, and she kissed him, soft, slow, somehow sensing he needed that, but a moment later he was Alejandro again, all fire and spirit, and strength and power, in control as ever. And she fell apart, holding on to him with the tips of her fingers, as though that might save her from what she knew was coming—what she'd now accepted as an inevitability of their relationship. She was falling all the way into love with him, and there was no use denying it, to herself at least.

'Cristo.' He pulled to stand, staring at her with a look in his eyes she couldn't comprehend—until gradually reality shifted and she understood what he was evidently dealing with.

'We forgot protection.' She winced. 'I didn't think—'

'I didn't give you a chance to think,' he dismissed. 'That was all my fault.'

She sat up, wrestling with a lingering sense of self-consciousness, her huge green eyes finding his. 'You know I'm on the pill.'

He dipped his head. 'It's not—'

'It is. In most cases, it's foolproof. And if anything happens, well, we'll cross that bridge when we get to it.'

He was going to argue with her, so she stood, pressing a hand gently to his chest. 'We can't undo it, so why worry? There's no point.'

He didn't argue with her, but she knew she hadn't completely dispelled his uneasiness. 'Dinner,' he murmured instead, looking around at their clothes—tossed destructively throughout the apartment.

'Right.' Her laugh was a soft sound. 'We were going out.'

'Is that what you want?'

What she wanted was more time with him. More than twelve hours, or whatever they had left. She felt the walls closing in on her and lifted her shoulders. 'Sure.' She couldn't meet his eyes. Emotion clogged in her chest.

Tell him.

'Alejandro—' But when he looked at her, he was so much like the first night they'd met—charming and untouchable—that her confidence faltered. Suddenly, *she* was like the night they'd met as well, nervous and unsure of herself, so she stood jerkily, wishing she weren't fighting a war within herself.

She *couldn't* love him. She never wanted to fall in love. She never wanted to get in a relationship—not like her parents'. Growing up with them had given her a crash course in how wrong things could go if you put all your trust in someone else's hands, and she never intended to be that stupid. Even if that someone was Alejandro Corderó? She tried to imagine him hurting her, tried to imagine him ever acting as her father had towards her mother, and she couldn't. The truth was, he was nothing like her father, so the boogieman fear she'd let dominate her all her life suddenly seemed a little ridiculous. Which meant what, exactly? That she was willing to take a risk?

But for what?

Even if she told him she wanted to see him again,

to date him out in the open, in a real way, he'd never agree. He'd been clear about that from the outset. It wasn't what he wanted.

And if that had changed? She squeezed her eyes shut as the dominoes kept falling, because it wasn't possible that he would have changed his mind *enough*. She needed to get married before she turned twenty-five and Alejandro was never going to be the marrying type. He might agree to more of this—no-strings sex—but that would be the extent of it. Which left her where, exactly? Falling more and more in love with a dedicated commitment-phobe while she really should have been looking for a man who would make a suitable husband?

It was all terribly, heart-stoppingly useless.

'I'm starving,' she lied, her voice over-bright.

His eyes narrowed thoughtfully, his eyes sweeping her face, but he didn't respond to the slightly brittle tone in her voice. 'Then I guess we'd better get you dressed once more.'

'Would you really have wanted to marry me, if I'd got pregnant after the wedding?'

After a long dinner in a buzzy restaurant in the fashionable Poblenou district, the question blurted from Sienna's lips before she could stop it.

To his credit, he didn't flinch. 'Yes.'

'Why?'

Her heart rabbited in her chest and she dug her nails into her thigh beneath the table, desperately willing her blood to stop rushing. 'Because I would want to be a part of my child's life.'

'That doesn't require marriage.'

'For me, it does.'

'Why?'

He finished his coffee, placing the small cup in the middle of the table then capturing her hands. 'Because I would want any child of mine to know that I was willing to fight to be a part of their everyday life. Not their weekend life. Not their sometimes life. All their life.'

She considered that, his vehemence a little discordant. 'Tell me about your father.'

As soon as she said it, she knew she'd struck a nerve. He flinched, almost imperceptibly, but her hand was held by his and she felt it, a little shock wave that passed through his body.

'There is nothing to tell. I never knew him.'

She frowned. 'Did your mother know? I mean—'

'Yes, she knew who he was.'

'And did she tell you?'

'Yes.'

'So you knew of him, but simply never met?'

He nodded once, a tight shift of his head that many would have taken as a warning: stop asking questions.

'Did he know about you?'

'Yes.'

'How do you know?'

'Because she told me.' His eyes were hooded, his features locked in a mask of ruthless anger. A shiver ran down her spine. 'And after she died, I found the letters.'

'She wrote to him?'

'A lawyer did. Some hack from the tenement. Still, the letter was sound. My father's legal advice was better— he had a team of barristers at his disposal.'

'He was well off?'

Alejandro lifted a hand in the air, silently signalling to the waiter that he'd like the bill—and, more importantly, signalling to Sienna that he wanted the conversation to be at an end.

'You ask too many questions.'

He had inflected the words with a hint of humour but that didn't matter. They hurt. They cut her to the quick. Criticism was something she'd thought she'd inured herself to—she'd learned to take it from her mother, but from Alejandro it was unbearable.

'That was a joke.' He sighed. 'Not a good one.' He squeezed her hand. 'I'm sorry.'

Apology. Another thing Sienna had never received—not from her mother, her father, and nor had she ever witnessed her father apologise to her mother. Alejandro might be six and a half feet of sheer alpha male, but he was also a decent, kind man, qualities her father lacked altogether.

'Forget about it.'

But neither of them could. She felt the sting of his words and it silenced any more questions. A moment later, the waiter appeared, and Alejandro paid the bill, despite Sienna's offer. 'You came to Barcelona. I can buy the dinner.'

'You're also hosting me,' she pointed out as they stepped out of the restaurant, into the balmy night air.

They walked in silence for several streets, moving towards the sea, the smell of salt growing stronger as they approached the water.

'My father,' he said, after so long a silence Sienna had presumed the conversation to be completely at an end, 'was in his early twenties when he met my mother.

She was working as a waitress. He was on vacation. He seduced her. He fed her lies, promised her things he never intended to give. She fell for him, believed him.'

Sienna's eyes stung with indignant tears. 'And she fell pregnant.'

'She was sixteen. She told him she was pregnant, he disappeared. She informed him of my birth—nothing. He gave her not a single cent towards my upbringing, nothing to help support her when I was a child. He refused the request for DNA testing. He abandoned her.'

He stopped walking, lifting a hand to her cheek. 'Do you wonder why I would have insisted on marrying you?'

A tingle ran through her. She swayed slightly—not intentionally, but because her legs seemed to have forgotten how to do their job. 'How could any man behave like that?'

'He was worried about the consequences of claiming me,' Alejandro said with a shrug, an air of assumed nonchalance not fooling Sienna for a minute.

'What consequences?'

'My father is an Italian count. His family fortune is considerable. I suppose he worried he might be disinherited. It is difficult to imagine how anyone could abandon a sixteen-year-old woman, but that's all I know.'

She blinked, anger firing through her. 'That's disgusting.'

Amusement quirked his lips, despite the seriousness of their conversation. 'Yes.'

'And now that you're Alejandro Corderó, world-famous success story, do you ever think about contacting him?'

'To what end?'

'Well, I don't know, but if I were you I'd have fantasised about tipping a drink or three over his head.'

Alejandro laughed, a sound that shook her to the core. 'Satisfying in the moment, but then again, why allow him to think that I care?'

'Don't you?'

His frown was reflexive. 'I care for the pain my mother endured—needlessly. I care for the life she should have lived, the care he could have given. He did not have to marry her, but he could have supported her financially.'

'And he could have known you. Loved you.'

He jerked his gaze away, looking towards the ocean. For a moment, he was a little boy again. She saw it, saw him, all the facets that made him the complex, fascinating man he was today. 'As a child, I wanted that. I needed it. But now, I need nothing from him.'

'Or anyone.' She hadn't meant to speak the words aloud, but somehow, she was glad she'd said them, because she needed the answer.

When he turned to face her, there was relief in his expression, as though she understood him and he was glad. 'Or anyone,' he repeated quietly, squeezing her hand. 'And I never will.'

There was a handful of people who knew how to access his penthouse without contacting him first. The concierge. Alejandro's driver, Raul. And Luca.

When Alejandro heard the door click open, some time before seven, when the smell of coffee had just started to fill the room, he tensed immediately, ready to fight, to defend, to protect Sienna, who was still sleeping down the corridor.

But the moment he saw Luca, different emotions knotted inside him. He remained tense.

'What are you doing here?'

Luca stood just inside the door, his dark eyes sweeping the apartment before landing on Alejandro. 'You have not been answering your phone. I was worried.'

A frown crossed his face. Where even was his phone? Usually, it was within arm's reach at all times, but since the night before he'd ignored it, wanting to blot out the world, the passing of time, everything. More than likely, it was charging in his bedroom.

'I didn't realise you were trying to contact me. Is everything all right?'

Luca prowled into the kitchen quietly, bracing his palms on the counter. His countenance had Alejandro worried. 'Probably.' He shrugged before fishing his own phone from the pocket of his dark jeans. 'Explain this.' He slid the device across the counter, and when Alejandro looked at it, something like lava poured down his throat.

'Where did you get this?'

'It ran in a gossip column a day ago.'

Alejandro couldn't take his eyes off the picture. Sienna had been so reluctant to dance, and yet there she was, in leather trousers, hair flaming down her back, body moving as though the music were running inside her bloodstream. He wanted to keep staring at it, but he was conscious of Luca and the implications of this photograph, and he felt the walls pushing in on him. The simple lie by omission was now an enormous canyon, and he stood right at the edge of it, precariously close to falling.

'It's Sienna, right?'

The idea of denying it didn't enter Alejandro's mind. It was one thing not to mention their relationship but quite another to lie to his best friend's face. Heat flushed his body as the reality of what they'd been doing slammed into him. He felt the sharp edge of the question, and badly wished Luca hadn't come here to ask it. But of course he had. What choice had Alejandro left him? His eyes flickered to the photo once more. Careless. Stupid. He should have taken better care of her. He'd failed Sienna, and Luca, and for the first time in a long time Alejandro grappled with a sense of wrongdoing.

'We connected at your wedding.'

'Connected?' Luca's voice was calm, but Alejandro felt the undercurrent of it. 'Is that all?'

'With all due respect, by what measure is that any of your business?' Only it was Luca's business. Sienna was his sister-in-law, and Luca was the only reason they'd met. More heat flushed through Alejandro now, as he imagined having *not* met Sienna. What if the wedding party had proceeded and he'd never noticed her? Never spoken to her? Never touched her? Ice overtook heat at a reality he refused to contemplate.

He turned away, his emotions firing, so he reached for the coffeepot and poured two dark, strong cups, handing one across to Luca even when he could barely meet the other man's eyes.

'You are aware of what she means to Olivia, and

what Olivia means to me. Sienna is therefore very much my business.'

Alejandro's gut twisted. And now, he felt like an outsider to their family, a wolf who'd abducted a feisty little sheep. 'But who she spends her time with is not.'

'You forget, Alex, I *know* how you spend your time. I know what you do to women. Please tell me you have not added her to the collection.'

Alejandro's fists pounded. Anger was a beast now, overtaking his body. 'What do I do to women?' he asked, the words dripping with contempt.

Luca waved a hand through the air. 'Nothing they don't welcome, but nor do you offer a chance for anything more than sex, and Sienna is not that kind of woman. She's been through too much to cope with you. She's not your equal in any way.'

The ground tipped beneath Alejandro's feet. He wanted to deny that, to defend her, but, God help him, Luca was right, and Alejandro had known it all along. Had known it and pursued this because he'd wanted her more than any other woman. Because she'd fascinated him—because of her differences from the women he usually slept with.

'Sienna's life is hers to live.'

Luca cursed, the sound filling the room, a loud, furious epithet. 'You are not denying it.'

'I'm saying it's none of your goddamned business.'

'And I'm saying it is. If you have used her, treated her badly, then you must know our friendship is at an end, Alex. She is Olivia's sister, which makes her my sister. My family.'

Alejandro drank from his coffee because he needed

the rush of adrenaline, but also because he needed to cool his temper. He was firing on all jets, and, despite what Luca had just said, they were close friends, and the friendship deserved to be handled with respect. But it was galling to hear Luca claim ownership over Sienna as though she were an object, instead of a fiercely intelligent woman with her own free will—who'd chosen him, and this.

'You shouldn't have come here.'

'I tried to contact you. When you didn't answer I thought one of two things: either something was wrong, or that you were avoiding me. Both warranted a personal visit.'

Alejandro made a sneering noise. 'I don't need to be mothered.'

'I'm not. If anything, I'm mothering Sienna.'

'She doesn't need it either.'

'How the hell would you know?'

Because I know her. Because I know that at her core there is strength and determination, because I see her like nobody else in the whole goddamned world does.

'Because she's a grown woman, capable of making her own choices.'

'And you are saying one of those choices was you?'

'I'm saying you should back the hell away from this.' Those protective instincts were back, raising Alejandro's hackles, so he wanted to push Luca out of his front door. 'Sienna's fine. I would never do anything to hurt her.'

'*Cristo.* It's true, isn't it? You screwed her?'

The crude expression jolted through Alejandro. 'At

any point have I ever discussed the intricacies of my personal life with you?'

'You don't need to. I've seen you in person. Which is why, when this photo came up on my phone, I knew there was more to it.'

'What the hell are you doing trawling gossip columns anyway? Don't you have more important things to be doing?'

'My assistant scans them each morning, looking for any mention of the pregnancy, or PR issues regarding the business.' He waved a hand through the air, dismissing the line of questioning. 'She sent the image, knowing my connection to you. How I happened to see it does not particularly matter, anyway.'

Alejandro compressed his lips, and for the first time since Luca arrived he was conscious of the fact that Sienna was in the room down the corridor, that if they were not careful she would wake and hear this argument. 'Come onto the terrace.' He gestured towards the space, the offer not exactly brimming with hospitality, but it was a stunning morning, and he hoped—

'I don't want to go onto the damned terrace, Alejandro. You're not listening to me. Sienna is not a plaything. She is not some bored socialite looking for a night of fun. She is a kind, gentle, sweet young woman who's been treated like you wouldn't believe by their mother for her whole life. I asked you to take care of her that night to *protect* her. Not just from her mother, but from any other guy who might make a pass at her. I asked you because I thought I could trust you—with my life.'

Guilt tore through Alejandro, splintering him into a thousand pieces. There was no defending what he'd done. Luca had relied on him and he'd betrayed him from the very first. But what about his obligations to Sienna, and to their chemistry? It had burned brightest of all, demanding attention. He had been split in two from the instant she'd turned towards him and blinked, as though she'd never seen a man before in her life. He'd focussed on their desire to the exclusion of all else, and yet his greatest fear was playing out right before him. He'd tried to make everything so clear, but what if he'd failed? What if he'd been inviting the same kind of mistreatment his father had meted out to his mother? What if he'd misled her into believing he could offer more? His goal in life was to avoid exploiting women, to prove to himself he was nothing like his father, and yet here he was, taking what he wanted from an innocent, inexperienced woman, using her body's desire for his justification. Guilt was a rush of arctic wind down his spine.

'You do not need to worry.' Except Alejandro *was* worried now.

'So this is not my wife's sister dancing with you? Or are you saying it was simply a dance, and nothing more?'

Scepticism laced the words and acid filled Alejandro's gut. 'I am not going to get into the details with you. If that is the only thing you're capable of speaking about, then perhaps it is better for you to leave.'

'Are you throwing me out?'

Alejandro ground his teeth together. Was she still asleep? *Cristo*, he hoped so. But just in case, he switched to his friend's native language. He knew Sienna spoke Spanish, but not Italian. At least if she heard the conversation, she wouldn't understand it. 'I'm not going to talk about Sienna any further.'

'Fine,' Luca responded in his own language seamlessly. 'Then let's talk about you. What in God's name did you think you were doing?'

CHAPTER THIRTEEN

SIENNA, ALREADY AWAKE, had dressed quickly when she'd heard voices, and now, as she padded softly, silently, down the hallway, she recognised Luca's.

'I asked you to look after Sienna. I asked you to flirt with her. To dance with her at the wedding. I specifically told you not to touch her, but you couldn't help yourself, could you? Despite the fact I hinted at her insecurities, her family problems, you just saw a willing woman and took her to bed? Accurate?'

They were speaking Italian, but it was one of the languages Sienna had tucked into her arsenal as a teenager. It was, in fact, her favourite. She heard the words without needing to pause and wonder what they meant, and they slammed into her like lead. Luca had *asked* Alejandro to flirt with her? To dance with her?

Her heart hammered against her ribs. Was that what that first night had been?

She pressed her back against the wall, terrified she might slump to the ground and that they'd find her as a big, blobby mess on the pristine floorboards. She squeezed her eyes shut, listening, concentrating on keeping her breathing quiet.

'And I did look after her.'

'You slept with her.'

Alejandro remained silent.

'Alejandro, I love you like a brother. I know you are a good man. But when it comes to women…'

'What? What do I do to women that is so bad?' She heard the hurt defensiveness in his voice and ached for him, because of how hard he tried to fix the lives of all the women who were like his mother.

'Nothing, when they are your usual type: rich, sophisticated women looking for a quick hit of pleasure and nothing more.'

'Do you know Sienna so well that you can say with certainty that she doesn't have those same feminine impulses and needs?'

Her stomach squirmed. She hated this. She hated being spoken about, she hated that they were fighting over her, but most of all she hated, in a way she doubted she could ever recover from, that Alejandro had been *babysitting* her the night they'd met. He'd walked away when they'd kissed and *she'd* chased *him*. She'd been chasing him all along, and now she'd foisted herself on him, in his own damned apartment. Never mind that he was obviously physically attracted to her: the conversation she was overhearing was evidence that he was physically attracted to any woman with a pulse. She was nothing special. But she'd made it impossible for him to say 'no', and he'd tried, several times.

'So you slept with her?'

'I'm not going to answer that.'

'I will take that as a yes.' Luca's voice was tight with tension. 'My God. Tell me this then—was it more than sex? Is that what's going on? Have you fallen in love with her? This would be the only way I could forgive you, you know. Love is different from sex—I understand its ability to change you, to alter what you want from life. Is that what happened?'

Silence stretched. Sienna's nerves pulled and she wanted, oh, how she wanted, to hear him admit that it was more than a physical thing. But after the longest pause Sienna had ever known, Alejandro's voice practically growled. 'We both know love isn't in my skill set.'

'So you don't care about her?'

The pause almost killed her. She held her breath, fingernails pressing into the palms of her hands as she waited, tortured, desperate; and then finally, he spoke.

'I care about her.' Her heart stumbled. 'She is, as you say, a beautiful, kind, sweet young woman. Of course I care about her, which is why you should not worry. I can promise you I have not done anything to hurt Sienna.'

But he was wrong. Pain squished her organs into a funny shape. She saw stars and the familiar sting of tears clawed at her throat.

'She has been starved for love by her parents, berated and belittled by her mother, insulted at every turn, so I am afraid she would be vulnerable to the first guy who showed any interest in her. Is that what you've done, Alejandro?'

Her heart dropped to her feet. Was this how Luca saw her? Olivia? How everyone saw her? How utterly pathetic. Was that what Alejandro had thought, when he'd come to speak to her at the wedding? Had he pitied her then? And when she'd approached him in Barcelona, was that why he'd eventually accepted? Because he felt *sorry* for her?

She was so hurt, and so angry, and she wasn't going to stand in the shadows and eavesdrop a second longer. They were wrong about her—all of them. She wasn't an object of pity—in fact, her pride had been hard fought and she would never let anyone take that away from her. 'I've heard enough.' Her voice came into the room with only the slightest wobble; she followed a moment later, glad she'd dragged on a pair of jeans and one of Alejandro's shirts, her hair pulled into a ponytail.

Luca whirled around, his expression unlike she'd ever seen it. She almost felt sorry for him. The panic in his eyes made her want to placate him, because she was every bit as soft-hearted as he'd accused her of being. But then she remembered how they'd been talking about her—Luca with such insulting, patriarchal pity and Alejandro with…cold detachment. She shivered, barely able to meet his look, though she felt his eyes on her, and couldn't fathom what he was feeling.

'Alejandro's right, Luca. This is none of your business.'

Luca's mouth dropped. 'I didn't know you were here.'

'No, and Alejandro doesn't know I speak Italian, so I can see why you each might have thought your conversation was nice and private.'

The words cut through the air. Luca's cheeks darkened. 'Listen, I'm sorry, I don't know what you heard…'

Now, she forced herself to meet Alejandro's eyes. Lightning sparked between them. 'I heard everything.'

Alejandro stayed right where he was, damn him. Didn't he know how badly she needed him? She wanted his arms to wrap around her, she wanted to feel his strength. But for all that she felt her own life slipping out of shape, she knew what she'd done to his as well. She'd put him in this position. She'd known he was Luca's best friend, and she'd pursued him, not caring how that might affect their relationship.

But he'd lied to her, and that was worse. How come he'd never told her that the only reason they'd met was because Luca had asked him to babysit her? Chagrin burned her cheeks pink. And yet, she wouldn't throw Alejandro to the wolves. His lie didn't change the fact that she'd pursued him. She'd come here asking him to make love to her. If Luca wanted to blame someone for the relationship, she was the rightful person.

'You're not giving your friend enough credit, Luca.' She dug her fingernails into the soft flesh of her palm to stave off tears. 'He tried to walk away from this. I pursued him. I wanted him. He did everything that was right and honourable. At no point has he ever misled me into thinking this is more than sex. Does that re-assure you?'

Luca dragged a hand through his hair. 'With respect, Sienna, you are no match for him. If he had truly wanted to walk away, he would have.'

'That is true.' Alejandro's voice reached her, wrapping around her, and she heard the hint of kindness in it. He was trying to make her feel better. To undo the hurt that had been pelting down on her. But it couldn't be undone. She'd lived through enough of that sting to know the way it landed in your soul and never shifted.

'More pity?'

His eyes narrowed; there was danger in their depths,

an anger and impatience that spoke of lost control. Not with her, but with Luca. He was furious with his friend for sparking this confrontation.

'Pity is irrelevant.'

'So you don't feel sorry for me?' She looked from one to the other, reality shifting to show her the truth for the first time since meeting Alejandro.

'I hate the way your mother treats you,' he said quietly. 'The way she spoke to you at the wedding…'

Luca looked from one to the other, a frown on his face, then he took a step nearer to Sienna. She ignored him.

'And so you slept with me to, what? Make me feel better?'

Luca swore softly.

Alejandro's only response was a visible one—his chest moved in and out, hard, as though he was struggling to draw breath.

'I don't need your pity.' Heat and hurt pride stung her cheeks. She turned to Luca. 'And I don't need you playing the part of the white knight, coming to save me from the big bad wolf or whatever. I appreciate that you're trying to protect Olivia from the fallout of this, from worrying about me, but I can assure you, there's no risk of that. She never needs to know about any of this.'

'I find it harder to contemplate misleading my wife than you two might.'

Sienna sucked in a jagged breath. 'I asked Alejandro to keep this a secret. Not because I wanted to "lie" to you and Olivia, but because my private life is exactly that—private. Olivia has been watching out for me since the day I was born and while I appreciate her to bits for that, it can be stifling, and I wanted to start living my damned life. Can't you see that this has nothing to do with you?'

'Even when I am the reason you met?'

'Because you asked him to look after me at the wedding?' Bile coated her throat. She didn't look at Alejandro.

Luca barely moved, but there was the slightest shift of his head, a small movement of acknowledgement.

'But everything that came after that was his decision and mine.'

'That's my point. Without me asking him to take care of you, none of this—'

'You don't get a say in what two consenting adults choose to do with their lives.' She dug her hands into her hips, her temperature spiking. 'I know you came here with good intentions, but I really think you should leave now. This is personal, and you don't need to get involved. I'm fine. Alejandro has made sure of that, all the way along.'

And he had. He'd been so careful to be honest with her, to keep her at arm's length during the day, making sure she understood that only the nights were hers, only his body.

But what of their dates? What of the way he'd shown her where he'd grown up? Wasn't that proof that he was sharing more than just his body? That maybe he wanted more from her?

She looked at him and her heart went cold, because she didn't see love in his eyes; she couldn't read anything there. Coldness flooded her soul.

'I'll leave. But I will stay downstairs, Sienna. When you're ready, you can come home with me.'

She had never felt more infantilised in her life. 'That won't be necessary.' He loved her sister so much, and he was doing everything he could to care for Sienna in Olivia's stead. She tried to soften her tone. 'Go home, Luca. I don't need you to protect me.' She moved closer to him, putting her hand on his forearm. 'But I do appreciate the sentiment.'

He grimaced, and she wondered if he was starting to rethink the wisdom of this.

'You, I will speak to later,' he muttered towards Alejandro, before stalking towards the door and leaving, so a crackling silence filled the room. Luca was gone, but his words were still there, ringing through the silence.

Alejandro watched her as though she were an unknown commodity, as though he couldn't predict how she might respond.

'Is that why you came up to me that night?'

The words throbbed with hurt she could no longer hide.

Alejandro's eyes closed for a moment and then he was moving towards her, but she flinched, needing him to stay far enough away so that she could continue to think.

'He asked you to "look out" for me?'

'Yes.'

At least he wasn't making up an excuse. 'And then, when I came to your office, you tried to get rid of me—'

'I did no such thing.'

'You did.' She wasn't interested in empty denials. 'But in the end, you took pity on me, because I was so honest, and you felt sorry for a woman like me, with no experience. You felt *sorry* for me.'

A muscle jerked in his jaw. 'Feeling sorry for you is not why I agreed to this.'

A sob was torn from her chest. 'No? Then why?'

'Because I *wanted* you,' he said firmly. 'Every part of you. I wanted you, despite the fact my best friend had told me I couldn't have you. I knew that being with you would jeopardise my friendship with Luca. Can you not see why I hesitated? He is like a brother to me, *querida*.'

She flinched. 'And can you not see how disgustingly patronising it is that you and he should even have had that conversation? To discuss me like…like…some kind of object that one of you has the right to grant permission to?' Heat stained her cheeks, anger rushing through her—anger was so much better than pain. 'You should have *told* me all of this. You should have told me it was why you stopped kissing me. You should have told me after we slept together. You should have told me when I asked you to keep our arrangement a secret. There were so many times when you could have explained why you'd come up to me that night…'

'But by then I knew you.' His words were spoken with devastating effect. 'I knew how others had treated you, I knew the dark voice of self-doubt that you have to work to combat, and I knew that you would take his remarks out of context.'

'Ah, is that what I'm doing?'

'Yes.'

'Really? So you don't think it matters that my brother-in-law begged you to "take care" of the poor, spinster sister? You can't see how that request reinforces every single rejection I've ever known in my life?'

His Adam's apple moved as he swallowed, and her eyes dropped to the gesture. Panic was gripping her, dragging her downwards. She dug her fingers into her hips to stave off the wave of nausea, fixing him with a frosty stare.

'But what does it matter, anyway? I came here because I wanted to learn about sex, and, regardless of all that, you've done an excellent job of teaching me what I wanted to know.'

His skin seemed to pale, his eyes probing hers, watching her with an intensity that made her shiver. She blinked, looking away.

'That's all this is, right? Sex? And now, we really don't have to see one another again, except in passing. At which point, you'll be civil, I'll be civil, and we'll pretend this never happened.'

'Sienna—'

'That's our agreement, right?'

'And that's what you want?'

What she wanted? She wanted to scream! What she wanted was the exact opposite of everything she'd just said, but how could she have any hope he would feel the same? Suppressing a curse, she pinned him with her eyes. 'What do *you* want, Alejandro?'

God, his name in her mouth still had the power to make her feel as though she'd ingested stars in their purest form.

'I want—I need—to know that he's wrong.' He came towards her then, each step making it harder for her to breathe. 'I want to know that I haven't hurt you. That this thing we've done hasn't hurt you.'

'Because you see me as he does. Weak. In need of protection. Well, I'm not. You might pity the way I was raised but you should also know this: it made me strong. I learned to cope with just about anything, thanks to my mother, so don't worry about hurting me. You don't have that power.' It was, of course, a lie. No one had quite the same power as Alejandro, but she couldn't reveal that to him. Not without revealing too much of her heart.

'Then why are you crying?'

She lifted her hands to her cheeks, dashing away the treacherous tears. 'Because I'm mad.'

'You should be.'

She crossed her arms over her chest. 'I'm sorry things between us are ending like this.'

'It doesn't have to end this way, though.'

She bit down on her lip, not daring to believe he was offering more. Not daring to believe he was going to suggest she stay.

'Don't think about what Luca said. Don't think about any of that. Remember how it felt in my arms. Remember how it felt to dance together, to walk together, to ride my bike together. This was more than either of us bargained for—that's the truth you should hold on to.'

'Why?'

He stared at her blankly.

'What good will it do to hold on to that truth? At the end of the day, it changes nothing. This was just sex. You don't want more from me than that.'

'Are you saying you want more from me?'

She felt the foolishness of her words—but too late.

It had been too easy for him to flip them back around on her. 'I— That's not an option.'

He watched her, waiting for her to continue. But what could she say? She needed to get married, and he'd never agree to that, unless of course she was pregnant, but what kind of marriage would that be? She shook her head slowly, clearing the thought—the hope and dream.

'I need to know I haven't hurt you.'

The words were dredged from the bottom of his soul and, finally, she understood. He lived in fear of becoming his father, of fooling a naïve, innocent woman into a relationship, of offering her more than he ever intended to give. He was terrified that history would repeat itself. It was why he'd worried so much about her potentially falling pregnant, why he'd been so adamant about marriage. And as hurt and angry as she was, she couldn't inflict those same wounds on him. He didn't deserve it. Or perhaps he did, but she loved him too much to be the instrument of pain to him.

'I'm fine, Alejandro. I got what I came here for, and now it's time for me to leave—just as we agreed. You've done an excellent job, everything I asked for, in fact. Please don't worry about me. I can't bear it.'

He frowned, scanning her face. 'And that's it?'

'What more do you want?'

She waited, so foolish to still hold hope in her heart, but wasn't that the power of love? To endlessly hope? It was the first time she'd understood her mother, and why she'd stayed with their father, even when he'd made her life a misery. She'd never lost hope that he would change, that one day he would give her what she needed, that he would love her back.

Sienna couldn't be like her. She wouldn't be. She gave up waiting.

CHAPTER FOURTEEN

SIENNA HAD BEEN wrong about hurt, and she'd been wrong about hope. Nothing in her past had prepared her for *this* kind of hurt, nothing protected her from its sting, and hope, damn it, hope was always there, beating its wings within her chest, so, no matter how she tried to push it aside, she felt it every time her phone buzzed, every time a car pulled up the drive of Hughenwood House, until, a month after leaving Barcelona, it was like embers in the woods rather than a proper flickering flame. Dying, but not dead, there within her, even when she knew it was impossible.

Alejandro Corderó was not the kind of man to pine after a woman. He wasn't sitting at home in Barcelona wishing she were with him. Hell, he wasn't thinking about her, remembering her, wanting her—he probably barely even remembered her name.

She knew that to be true, and she'd known it from the moment they'd got involved, but that didn't stop the pain from seeping into her organs, her cells, her blood until it was a thriving part of her.

'Really, Sienna? Pink and purple? You seem to have forgotten you're not an eight-year-old anymore.'

Sienna looked down at the dress she'd chosen—a summery, cotton shift in big bright splotches, and lifted her shoulders, pretending her mother's words didn't cut deep into her chest.

'And with your hair? Perhaps I should get you checked for colour blindness.'

She ground her teeth together. 'I'm taking Starbuck for a walk.'

'It's going to rain.'

'I don't mind.'

'Suit yourself.'

Sienna snapped her fingers and Starbuck came bounding into the room, a big, happy smile for Sienna and a growl for Angelica Thornton-Rose. Angelica grimaced in the dog's direction then turned, sashaying out of the kitchen as though the tiles were her own personal runway.

Sienna didn't walk far. She couldn't. She was so tired. In the first few days since leaving Spain, she'd been possessed by a form of manic energy, so she'd cleaned the house from top to bottom, pruned the orchard and replanted the vegetable patch, but as the reality of what she'd lost had sunk in she'd felt her energy deplete completely, and every day she woke with the same sense of dread in her belly: how was she going to get through this without him?

Alejandro shrugged off the woman's hand before turning to face her. The bar was dark, the music muted, the crowd thick. It was the perfect place to be alone—which was what he wanted.

'Alex, hi,' she purred, her pink lacquered nails catching the down lights, making them shimmer. She lifted one to her lip, tracing the outline of the lower. 'How've you been?'

He grunted in response, turning back to his drink.

'That good, huh?' She leaned closer, her perfume intoxicating. 'I've got some ideas for how you can feel better.'

He vaguely remembered her. They'd slept together a couple of years ago, after meeting at the opening of a nightclub. Her name escaped him.

'I'm not interested.'

'That's because you haven't heard my ideas yet.' And she kissed him just beneath his earlobe, a possessive hand pressing to his chest, so he stood abruptly, dislodging her completely.

'I'm not interested.'

She stared at him, bemused. And could he blame her? He had earned the reputation he had as a womaniser, a devoted bachelor. No wonder she thought he was a sure thing.

'Excuse me.'

He threw some money on the bar to cover his tab then stalked out, one hand in his pocket, curled around the emerald necklace that had, for a brief time, hung so close to her breasts and heart, a necklace he'd found curled carefully on the bedside table after she'd left.

His head was bent low and his heart raced. Because he hadn't been with anyone since Sienna, and though he'd contemplated it, wondering if it might be what he needed to put her out of his head, he now had his answer: when the other woman had touched him, he'd wanted to hurl. Sex with anyone else wasn't the answer. So what was?

'I'm so happy for you guys.' Sienna hugged Olivia close, her eyes meeting Luca's over her sister's shoulder. He had the decency to look ashamed.

'Thanks. I wanted to wait until I saw you in person to tell you. Can you believe it? A baby!'

'Wonderful news.' Sienna nodded, mustering what she hoped would pass for an enthusiastic smile to her face as Olivia spoke almost nonstop about her pregnancy and excitement, about where they planned to live and how she wanted to decorate the nursery, and, in the small part of her mind still capable of functioning, Sienna saw for herself that Olivia and Luca were clearly besotted with one another. There was nothing fake about their relationship. Nothing contractual. They were in love. Genuine, mutual love.

Tears crowded her throat and she smiled, hoping they'd pass for happy tears. 'Congratulations. Have you told Mum?'

'I think I'll save that pleasure for another day.' Olivia looked from Luca to Sienna, as if for courage. 'Actually, speaking of Mum, there's something I wanted to talk to you about.'

'Oh?'

'There's an apartment in Rome. Luca…um…gave it to me, and we're not using it, so I wondered if you'd consider moving in?'

She stared at her sister in confusion. 'But why?'

'Well, because I miss you, for one thing, and because

once the baby's born, I'll want you close. But also, because it gets you out of here.'

They both looked around the cavernous lounge room of Hughenwood House.

More pity.

'I'm okay, Libby. I've lived here all my life. I know how to deal with it.'

'But I miss you.'

'I miss you too. I'll come visit, I promise.'

'We would enjoy having you close by.' Luca's deep voice shifted between them. An apology? A hope of smoothing over the past?

She lifted her shoulders. 'I'll think about it.'

And on the one hand, she was tempted. She adored Olivia, and missed her like crazy. The thought of being close to her, particularly with her now being pregnant, was like a talisman that Sienna found it hard to turn away from. But it was also an escape route that only a coward would pursue. She couldn't run away from her life, not really. Even in Italy, the past would follow, and the ache she felt at missing Alejandro would still be there, right in the middle of her heart.

Five weeks. He stared at the pool, the glistening water, remembering her, seeing her, the visage of Sienna so freaking real in his mind that she might as well have been there right now. He reached out a hand, but there was nothing. No Sienna. No hope. His gut twisted.

This was what they'd agreed to.

So why the hell couldn't he move on?

The way she'd looked on that last morning, when she'd put two and two together and come up with eight—that she could actually believe their relationship had boiled down to pity. That he'd slept with her because he felt sorry for her! He'd wanted her so badly, so much that it had been eating through him, between the wedding party and when she'd arrived at his office in Barcelona. She thought he'd agreed because he'd felt sorry for her? He'd agreed because he'd felt as though his life depended on it.

There was no pity there. Nothing but need.

And suddenly, it was imperative that she comprehend that. He didn't know why, but it was vitally important that Sienna not be existing with the idea in her mind that anything other than desire had motivated him to be with her.

He'd wanted her, and so he'd taken her—with no regard for the consequences. But that didn't mean there weren't any—and how would he know? He hadn't spoken to her since. He had no idea what her life was like, what she felt, if she was okay and, more importantly, he didn't know if their passionate affair had resulted in any complications. He owed it to her to find out.

She stared at her phone, disbelief curling in her gut, and she reached for it quickly, before her mother could see Alejandro's face on the screen and ask a barrage of questions Sienna had no intention of answering.

'Hello?'

'Sienna.'

Her name on his lips was like a whisper. She closed her eyes, moving from the dining room without looking at her mother. Starbuck padded along beside her.

'Is everything okay?' She pressed her back against

the timber-panelled walls of the hallway, her eyes fixed on one of the paintings across from her.

'I'm outside. Do you have a moment?'

'What do you mean, outside? Outside, where?'

'Your home.'

She startled, pushing off the wall and moving towards the front door. 'My home in England?'

'Yes.'

'But why?'

'Could you come out? Or let me in?'

Her heart went into overdrive. 'I'll— Just a moment.' She disconnected the call, her pulse firing like crazy, her eyes running over her reflection in the hall mirror before she wrenched the door inwards. He was a little way across the drive, his back to her, the darkness of the night making it difficult to see much more than his frame. His large, strong frame. A body that had possessed her and driven her wild. A body she had foolishly started to think of as 'hers'.

She closed the door behind herself, Starbuck at her heels as she walked towards him on legs that felt made of jelly. Every step was the beating of a drum, slow, over and over, reaching into her soul, until her footsteps alerted him and he turned to face her and her world tilted wildly off its axis. Her heart beat way too fast. She couldn't do this. She was so completely in love with him that seeing him like this just made her want to fall to the ground and weep.

But she had to be strong. Not for ever, just for the next few minutes.

'I had to know.'

She shook her head, frowning. 'What do you need to know?' The words were barely a whisper.

'Are you—' But he didn't speak. He moved closer, their bodies almost touching, his gaze devouring her face in that way he had, so she closed her eyes, their past so perfect that to contemplate it was to experience a deep, sharp sense of pain. He smelled of his cologne, but there was the undertone of liquor, Scotch or vodka, something strong, so she frowned. He'd driven here, so he couldn't be drunk, but she could smell it on his breath…

'Your last night in Barcelona. That dress. When we didn't use—' His face contorted and his pain was like a whip, slicing through her.

'I'm not pregnant.' She blurted out the words, pressing a hand to her flat stomach regardless, ignoring the strange wave of longing that dragged on her. 'So you don't have to worry about that.'

'I see.' But he didn't move. He didn't step back, and his face didn't relax. Every line in his body was taut with tension. She knew she should put space between them but being close to him was hypnotic and necessary, after more than a month apart. She'd missed him so much.

And he'd only come to make sure she wasn't pregnant. He just wanted reassurance that he never needed to see her again, that was all. Fool! She cursed herself for allowing hope to catch hold of her.

'That's good.' But his voice sounded heavy. She didn't understand why he wasn't jumping for joy. He took a step backwards then, lifting a hand to his head, dragging fingers through his hair.

'Is that all you wanted?'

He pinned her with sparkling grey eyes. 'No.'

'Oh.' She braced herself for whatever was to follow. The truth was, she wasn't strong enough for this. She wanted to be. She wanted to feel nothing, but instead she felt too much. A river of emotions was coursing through her body, transforming her, so she found it impossible to fight this.

'That morning, with Luca…'

She swallowed, the words she'd overheard burned into her brain.

'I need to explain.'

'No, you don't,' she cut him off unevenly. Because nothing he said could fix it, and there was no point in trying. 'It doesn't matter.'

'It matters to me,' he growled, so Starbuck trotted over from where she'd been tinkering with a dropped apple. He softened his voice. 'Indulge me, for two minutes.'

Sienna looked towards the house and shivered. Only her lonely life and mother awaited her up there. 'Fine.' She tried to brace her heart for whatever would follow.

'Luca asked me to look after you, and, yes, he prohibited me from touching you. I appreciate how that must make you feel. In hindsight, I should have questioned him on the spot, but I didn't *know* you then. I wanted to help my best friend. Who you were was somewhat irrelevant.'

'Thanks.'

He grimaced. 'Let me finish.' She nodded jerkily, but her pulse was on fire, her throat hurt—everything hurt, in fact. 'From the moment I met you, I was waging a war, between what Luca had asked of me and what I wanted. At first, I thought you were like any other woman, that I wanted you because that's what I *do* when I meet a beautiful woman, but that's not true. You got under my skin, Sienna. Even then, on that first night, you bewitched me, with your two left feet and quick tongue, so I had to know more, to understand you completely. I wanted you—just you—and Luca had nothing to do with that.'

She tilted her chin, refusing to believe him, refusing to allow her heart to be vulnerable to him again. 'That's who you are. You said it yourself, you see a woman and you seduce her.'

'Not you. Not that night.'

'Because I wasn't your "usual" type?'

'Right.'

She sucked in a hurt, sharp breath.

'Because you were better,' he insisted angrily. 'You were so much more than any person I'd ever met. Have you ever had the sense that everyone in the world is like a shadow? I'd been so bored, Sienna, so restless, until I met you and you brought everything into focus for me.'

'You regretted sleeping with me.'

'Do you blame me? I'd wanted you, but I knew what that would mean to Luca, if he ever found out. I couldn't tell him—that would betray you—and so I knew I had to hide the truth, that I would have to live with the guilt of betraying him.'

'My sex life has nothing to do with my brother-in-law,' she shouted, so Starbuck weaved between her legs and made a low, reproachful growling noise towards Alejandro. She patted the dog's head to calm her.

'I know that. The situation was complicated. I resolved to leave you alone, even though I thought of you every night.'

'Oh, come on, Alejandro. I might have been a virgin but I'm not that naïve. I know what you're like. I'm sure you found ways to console yourself after the wedding, other women to distract yourself with.'

'No,' he denied vehemently. 'There has been no one since I met you. I went out with some women, in a stupid, misguided attempt to push you from my mind, but I did not so much as touch my companions. I couldn't. I craved *you*, Sienna, and anyone else would have been a very poor substitute.'

'Am I supposed to be flattered by that?' Her voice shook, because the truth was she didn't know what to make of his confession, but it did succeed in touching something deep inside her.

'I'm just trying to explain why I hesitated. You arrived in my office and I wanted to rip your clothes off your body, but I'd been living with guilt, trying to balance what I'd promised Luca, what I knew about you, with what you and I both wanted. I walked a tightrope the entire time together, but that doesn't change the fact that being with you was the most meaningful thing I've ever done.'

She spun away from him, no longer able to see him, to hear him. It was too much. Tears spilled down her cheeks, thudding against her breasts. She dashed them away but more sprang up, rolling with abandon over her face.

'I wanted you. For you. Nothing else mattered. And yet I'd spent my whole life convinced that I would never fall in love, never get married, never live a normal life. I sure as hell never wanted to be depended on, to let someone love me. Do you think any of that mattered? Intentions don't mean a damn, it turns out, when it comes to love.'

She stopped walking and dropped her head, not trusting her brain to properly decode what he was saying, not trusting herself to hope.

'I tried so hard not to love you, but what hope did I have? From the first moment we met, my heart was yours, and I know it will be always, whether you come home to Spain with me or not.'

She was shivering uncontrollably, his words rolling through her, but there was panic too, and despair, because she'd made herself a promise as a teenager and she couldn't think of abandoning it. 'I can't.' She sobbed.

'Right.' He nodded once, surprise in his eyes, but it was quickly hidden behind a mask of calm. 'I expected that would be your answer, but I needed to tell you. These last few weeks, it's been building like a weight on top of me, so all I could think of was telling you how I feel. I love you. I need you in my life.'

'And I need to get married, and I know that's not something you'll ever want, and I accept that. I knew it about you from the start, but it's only going to get harder to leave you if we prolong this. You're not the only one who's struggled these last six weeks. I have been devastated. You talk about the world growing bright? All the lights have gone out for me. I've barely been existing. What would that feel like in a month's time? In six months? When you get sick of me and realise that your first impulse was right, that you're not into celibacy and happily ever after? I can't do it. I can't walk away from you again.'

'You misunderstand me. I'm not asking you to walk away. I'm asking you to walk into my arms and stay there for the rest of your life. I'm asking you—no, I'm begging you to marry me, Sienna. Whenever, wherever you would like. I cannot imagine my life without you in it.'

She pressed a hand to her mouth, to stop her sob from ringing out through the orchard.

But could she really hope this was happening? Could she really trust him?

'I thought Luca was crazy. He and I have always hated the idea of marriage, but now I see how stupid I've been. Marriage is irrelevant—it's the person you pledge to spend your life with, and all I can think about is wanting you with me. I want to shower you in love, to dote on you, to sleep with you over and over and over again, to work with you, to see you take my charity and turn it into something that changes the world. I want to *live* with you, to live my life, spend my days, enriched by you and supporting you. Not because I pity you. I never have. But because I need you, and I love you, and, frankly, I worship you.'

How could she answer? How could she find words?

'I thought of you as soon as I saw this.' He reached into his pocket, pulling out the emerald necklace. 'It is just like you—strong, unique, elemental and perfect.' He reached into his other pocket, removing another velvet pouch. 'But then I saw this, and I knew I couldn't come here without bringing it, regardless of your answer.'

He handed it to her and as their fingertips brushed a rush of heat spread through her body, tightening her stomach. She tilted it into her hand without looking, just as she had the first time he'd given her jewellery. But the weight of this demanded her attention, and when she looked down it was to see the most enormous solitaire diamond, surrounded by a circlet of black diamonds.

'My answer? I'm not sure I heard you actually ask a question.'

He lifted a brow, and for the first time since arriving he looked like himself. Almost relaxed, even.

'You're right, of course. How foolish of me.' He dropped to one knee, right in front of her, and Starbuck gave him an affectionate sniff. Alejandro laughed gruffly, patting the dog's head, before lifting a hand to Sienna's and holding it in his. 'I came here to explain, but mainly, I came to tell you that I love you and that all I can think about, all I've wanted for a long time, is for you to become my wife. Sienna Thornton-Rose, would you consider marrying me?'

She was silent, not because she didn't want to speak, but because she struggled to find the words.

'You don't have to answer straight away.' He stood, the relaxation gone, hesitation replacing it, so she ached all over because she loved him so much, and he was still suffering, with no idea how she felt.

'I can't,' she explained in a rush, so he nodded, his shoulders tense as he took a backwards step.

'Right.'

'No.' She laughed unevenly. 'I mean, I can't answer

straight away. I don't know how to. That is to say, I don't know—you were so eloquent, and I have no words, I just know that I want—that I—' She shook her head in frustration.

He moved closer, taking the ring from her hand and fixing his eyes to hers. 'Do you love me?'

She nodded slowly. 'With all my heart.'

'I know I'm not the kind of man you intended to marry, but do you think you could—'

'I only want to marry you.' She rushed out the words. 'I can't imagine ever, *ever* being with another man. You're saving me from a life of celibacy,' she said with an upward tilt of her lips.

'I cannot picture you as a nun.'

'But a wife?'

'My wife? Definitely.'

In the end, when she and Alejandro were married, Luca and Olivia by their sides, Sienna's father's will was the furthest thing from her mind. As were her father, her mother and the lifetime of insults she'd been made to bear.

Her heart and soul were full of her husband, their future, their promise to one another, and the certainty that she was exactly where she was meant to be. Life was good, and Sienna had every expectation that it always would be, so long as there was love, and Alejandro.

* * * * *

Couldn't get enough of
Forbidden Nights in Barcelona*?*
You're sure to love the first instalment in
The Cinderella Sisters duet
Vows on the Virgin's Terms

And why not also catch these other
Clare Connelly stories?

Their Impossible Desert Match
An Heir Claimed by Christmas
Cinderella's Night in Venice
My Forbidden Royal Fling
Crowned for His Desert Twins

Available now!

WE HOPE YOU ENJOYED
THIS BOOK FROM
⊞ HARLEQUIN
PRESENTS

Escape to exotic locations where passion knows no bounds.

Welcome to the glamorous lives of royals and billionaires, where passion knows no bounds. Be swept into a world of luxury, wealth and exotic locations.

8 NEW BOOKS AVAILABLE EVERY MONTH!

#3985 BOUND BY HER RIVAL'S BABY
Ghana's Most Eligible Billionaires
by Maya Blake

Why, wonders Amelie, does she feel such a wild attraction to Atu? He wants to buy her family's beach resort, so he's completely off-limits. Yet surrendering to their heat was inevitable...and now she's pregnant with his heir!

#3986 THE ITALIAN'S RUNAWAY CINDERELLA
by Louise Fuller

Talitha's disappearance from his life has haunted billionaire Dante. Now he'll put their relationship on fresh footing—by hiring her to work for him. Yet with their chemistry as hot as ever, will he ever be able to let her go again?

#3987 FORBIDDEN TO THE POWERFUL GREEK
Cinderellas of Convenience
by Carol Marinelli

The secret to Galen's success is his laser-sharp focus. And young widow Roula is disruption personified! Most disruptive of all? The smoldering attraction he can't act on when he hires her as his temporary assistant!

#3988 CONSEQUENCES OF THEIR WEDDING CHARADE
by Cathy Williams

Jess doesn't know what she was thinking striking a just-for-show arrangement to accompany notorious playboy Curtis to an A-List wedding. What will the paparazzi uncover first—their charade...or that Jess is now expecting his baby?

#3989 THE BILLIONAIRE'S LAST-MINUTE MARRIAGE
The Greeks' Race to the Altar
by Amanda Cinelli

With his first bride stolen at the altar, Greek CEO Xander needs a replacement, fast! Only his secretary Pandora—the woman he holds responsible for ruining his wedding day—will do... But her touch sparks unforeseen desire!

#3990 THE INNOCENT'S ONE-NIGHT PROPOSAL
by Jackie Ashenden

After everything cynical Castor has witnessed, there's almost nothing he's surprised by. But naive Glory's offer to sell him her virginity floors him! Of course, it's out of the question. Instead, he makes a counter-proposal: become his convenient bride!

#3991 THE COST OF THEIR ROYAL FLING
Princesses by Royal Decree
by Lucy Monroe

Prince Dimitri's mission to discover who's leaking palace secrets leads him to an incendiary fling with Jenna. As their connection deepens, could the truth cost him the only woman that sees beyond his royal title?

#3992 A DEAL FOR THE TYCOON'S DIAMONDS
The Infamous Cabrera Brothers
by Emmy Grayson

Anna has spent years healing from her former best friend Antonio's rejection. Then a dramatic fall into the billionaire's arms spark headlines. And his solution to refocus the unwanted attention? A ruse of a romance!

YOU CAN FIND MORE INFORMATION ON UPCOMING HARLEQUIN TITLES, FREE EXCERPTS AND MORE AT HARLEQUIN.COM.

HPCNMRB0122B

Why, Amelie wonders, does she feel such a wild attraction to Atu? He wants to buy her family's beach resort, so he's completely off-limits. Yet surrendering to their heat was inevitable...and now she's pregnant with his heir!

Read on for a sneak preview of
Maya Blake's next story for Harlequin Presents
Bound by Her Rival's Baby

A breeze washed over Amelie and she shivered.

Within one moment and the next, Atu was shrugging off his shirt.

"Wh-what are you doing?" she blurted as he came toward her.

Another mirthless twist of his lips. "You may deem me an enemy, but I don't want you catching cold and falling ill. Or worse."

She aimed a glare his way. "Not until I've signed on whatever dotted line you're determined to foist on me, you mean?"

That look of fury returned. This time accompanied by a flash of disappointment. As if he had the right to such a lofty emotion where she was concerned. She wanted, no, *needed* to refuse this small offer of comfort.

To return to her room and come up with a definite plan that removed him from her life for good.

So why was she drawing the flaps of his shirt closer? Her fingers clinging to the warm cotton as if she'd never let it go?

She must have made a sound at the back of her throat, because his head swung toward her, his eyes holding hers for an age before he exhaled harshly.

His lips firmed and for a long stretch he didn't speak. "You need to accept that I'm the best bet you have right now. There's no use fighting. I'm going to win eventually. How soon depends entirely on you."

The implacable conclusion sent icy shivers coursing through her. In that moment she regretted every moment of weakness. Regretted feeling bad for invoking that hint of disappointment in his eyes.

She had nothing to be ashamed of. Not when vanquishing her and her family was his sole, true purpose.

She snatched his shirt from her shoulders, crushing her body's instant insistence on its warmth as she tossed it back to him. "You should know by now that threats don't faze me. We're still here, still standing after all you and your family have done. So go ahead, do your worst."

Head held high, she whirled away from him. She made it only three steps before he captured her wrist. She spun around, intent on pushing him away.

But that ruthlessness was coupled with something else. Something hot and blazing and all-consuming in his eyes.

She belatedly read it as lust before he was tugging her closer, wrapping one hand around her waist and the other in her hair. "This stubborn determination is admirable. Hell, I'd go so far as to say it's a turn-on, because God knows I admire strong, willful women," he muttered, his lips a hairsbreadth from hers, "but fiery passion will only get you so far."

"And what are you going to do about it?" she taunted a little too breathlessly. Every cell in her body traitorously strained toward him, yearning for things she knew she shouldn't want but desperately needed anyway.

He froze, then with a strangled sound leaving his throat, he slammed his lips onto hers.

He kissed her like he was starved for it. *For her.*

Don't miss
Bound by Her Rival's Baby,
available March 2022 wherever
Harlequin Presents *books and ebooks are sold.*

Harlequin.com